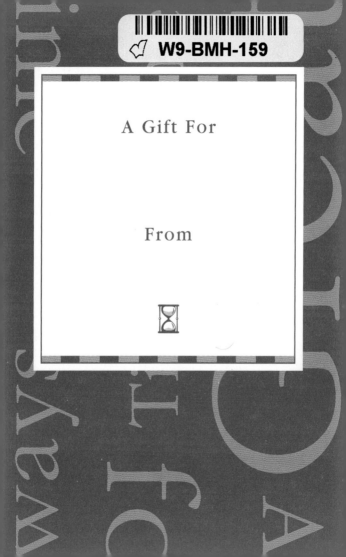

A Gift For

From

THERE'S ALWAYS TIME FOR GREATNESS

FOR GREATNESS

WHO DID WHAT WHEN

FROM AGES 1–100

There's Always Time for Greatness

for Greatness

Who Did What When, from Ages 1 to 100

Andrew Postman

Illustrated by Nick Galifianakis

For all ages. Literally.

BOOKS

William Morrow
An Imprint of HarperCollins *Publishers*

Library of Congress Cataloging-in-Publication Data

Postman, Andrew.
    What's in an age? : who did what when, from age 1 to 100 / Andrew
Postman : illustrated by Nick Galifianakis.
        p.   cm.
    "For all ages. Literally."
    ISBN: 0-688-16911-2
    1. Biography—Miscellanea.   I. Title.
CT105.P67   1999
920—dc21   99-19714
            CIP

Printed in the United States of America

First Edition

3 4 5 6 7 8 9 10

www.williammorrow.com

Introduction

Put the gun down.

This book is *not* intended to show you (or me) what losers we are, how little we've accomplished when compared with the most celebrated examples of humankind. So put the cap back on the bottle. This book isn't meant to kindle that hangdog feeling that moved singer-songwriter Tom Lehrer, at age 37, to note that "when Mozart was my age, he had been dead for two years." Frankly, it's *encouraging* that we're all so schooled in the oddity of Mozart's precociousness (composing his first symphony at age 8, for instance). Why encouraging? Well, if we lived in a world where 8-year-old symphony composers weren't freakish but commonplace, then those of us who weren't penning at least rondos during our second-grade lunch breaks would *really* have something to get down about.

So shut off the oven.

Granted: Except for the most evolved among us (and aren't they just too perfect), we all obsess over how we stack up—creatively, professionally, financially, socially, even spiritually—against our fellow human beings. And age is perhaps the most obvious and natural measuring stick, allowing us instantly to gauge how to spin what we've done so far. Damn that acquaintance of yours for becoming partner in her law firm—not because she got to be partner, but because she's two years younger than you and you're not there yet. Whether or not we acknowledge it, we create in our minds certain benchmarks we aspire to—for example, new bicycle by age 10, varsity letter by 15, carnal knowledge by 20, professional focus by 25, marriage by 30, parenthood by 35, solvency by 40, fame by 50, Kennedy Center Lifetime Achievement Award by 60, etc. Every life is unique, and no two sets of circumstances are identical, yet we often look to those who are our age as if we've been running in the same race, and it is against their progress, good (e.g., Pulitzer Prize) or bad (jail time), that we set our mood. Does the following thought—which has actually passed through my own brain—sound familiar? *Bill Gates may be worth approximately $80 billion more than I am, but he is six years older (always will be), so I have a chance to catch up, or even pass him, once I set my mind to it.*

I didn't say it was sane.

Why do we do compare like this? Insecurity? Sure. But there's more to it than that. When we lift our heads to look at the surrounding landscape, we need a horizon to focus on. Age is that horizon, a leveler. It brands people immediately. Our sense of a life is seasoned by what's been accomplished by a given age, and conversely, we judge accomplishments by the age at which they were achieved. Nothing gives context like a person's years.

This book is a celebration—and, I hope, an illumination—of human accomplishment, and occasional folly, at every age from 1 to 100. There are the early birds (monarchs and entertainers seem to reign here) and those who take their sweet time to make their mark (great novelists—Jane Austen and F. Scott Fitzgerald excluded—generally don't kick into gear until after 30). There are the late bloomers (note the abundance here of politicians and—strangely—fast-food magnates: Ray Kroc didn't start the McDonald's chain until he was 52, while Colonel Harland Sanders founded Kentucky Fried Chicken at 65). Great inventions and scientific and medical insights have often emerged from younger minds, but much of the world's finest architecture and the birth of many socially progressive movements have come to life thanks to more experienced women and men. (Not, by the way, that age automatically equals wisdom: See Neville Chamberlain, age 69, for proof that some people don't, in fact, get better with age.)

You'll find those whose brilliance was packed into a short period (Keats, van Gogh), and those who managed consistently amazing feats over many decades (Michelangelo, Ben Franklin). The man who gave us Twinkies is here, and the one who gave us Silly Putty. I have included the woman who first described cystic fibrosis and the girl who made Lourdes a destination for the wounded and wandering.

So why did I choose the entries I chose? Because they were

§ **world-altering events** (Man Walks on the Moon, age 38; Assassin Ignites World War I, age 19) and red-letter artistic and scientific achievement (the writing of *Hamlet,* the painting of the *Mona Lisa*, the discovery of radium).

❧ **achievers and achievements** from a range of eras, places, and disciplines.

❧ **offbeat and smaller** (but perhaps no less enduring) **achievers**. For example, the authors of both "Twinkle, Twinkle, Little Star" and "Happy Birthday to You" get recognition here alongside Handel and his *Messiah*.

But perhaps the more pressing question I need to answer is this: Why are certain great accomplishments and their accomplishers *not* included?

❧ **The accomplishment didn't take place at one discernible moment.** For example, Constantine the Great may have done more than any individual to help spread Christianity and allow Western civilization to flower, but there is no instant, among his extraordinary contributions, as singular as, say, Martin Luther's nailing of the 95 theses on the door of Wittenberg Cathedral at the age of 33.

❧ **The accomplishment is overshadowed by a similar, more notable accomplishment**. For example, Beethoven and Brahms were each working on their final, most spectacular symphonies (the ninth for Ludwig, the fourth for Johannes) at age 52. To leave room for the nonsymphonic achievement of some other 52-year-old, I chose—sorry, Johannes—to include only one of these great works. (Note: The ninth wasn't finished and performed until Ludwig was 53.)

You will not come away from this book thinking what a loser you are (unless, perhaps, you were thinking that before you even saw this book, in which case I can't help you). More likely, you will feel inspired, intrigued, surprised by what you learn. I know that in researching this book I felt all those things.

So step down from the chair. Unknot the rope. This will not take years off your life.

—Andrew Postman
January 1999

THERE'S ALWAYS TIME
FOR GREATNESS

WHO DID WHAT WHEN

FROM AGES 1–100

At the Age of 0–1 . . .

Mary, of the House of Stuart, becomes Queen of Scotland.

Hercules strangles two serpents placed in his cradle.

Mickey Rooney debuts in the family vaudeville act.

Jesus is visited in a manger.

. . . **Brooke Shields is selected the Ivory Snow baby.**

At the Age of 2 . . .

Tenzin Gyatso is declared the 14th (and present) Dalai Lama.

Judy Garland launches her stage career.

Hsuan-t'ung becomes Emperor of China (the final one).
Isabella II ascends to the Spanish throne.

It is often hard to get along with a child between two and three.

—DR. BENJAMIN SPOCK,
COMMON SENSE BOOK OF BABY AND CHILD CARE

Isaac Asimov rips out each page of a book as he turns it, then grows very sad to see the book empty. (He will go on to write roughly 500 books.)

At the Age of 3 . . .

Tiger Woods shoots 48 for 9 holes on his hometown golf course in Cypress, California.

Alice Liddell first meets Charles Dodgson (pen name: Lewis Carroll), who will use her as inspiration to write *Alice's Adventures in Wonderland*.

Albert Einstein speaks for the first time.

> **Ordinarily, we do not expect a child to show any fear of the dark until he has reached the age of three.**
>
> —DR. DOUGLAS A. THOM,
> *EVERYDAY PROBLEMS OF THE EVERYDAY CHILD*

Ernest Hemingway receives his first fishing rod.

Ivan the Terrible becomes Grand Prince of Moscow.

At the age of four years and eight months, Louis XIV, King of France and Navarre, was not merely the master but also the owner of the goods and bodies of nineteen million men, given into his power by a decree of the almighty.

—PHILIPPE ERLANGER, *LOUIS XIV*

At the Age of 4 . . .

Kim Ung-Yong, with an estimated IQ of 200, speaks fluent Korean, English, Japanese, and German.

Andre Agassi hits tennis balls for 15 minutes with Jimmy Connors, then the world's top player.

Alastair Grahame inspires his father, Kenneth, to make up a bedtime story, which turns into *The Wind in the Willows*.

Louis XIV becomes King of France, upon the death of his father, Louis XIII.

Natasha Richardson appears in the film *The Charge of the Light Brigade,* starring her mother (Vanessa Redgrave) and directed by her father (Tony Richardson).

Malcolm Little—who later changes his name to Malcolm X—watches as his family's home is burned down by members of the Ku Klux Klan.

Bob Hope emigrates from England to the United States.

. . . Beatrice d'Este has her hand offered in marriage
by her father to the Duke of Bari, age 29.
(They will marry 11 years later.)

At the Age of 5 . . .

Debora Wilson, mountain climber, scales a 4,000-foot peak.

Christopher Robin Milne hears the first "Winnie-the-Pooh" story, with himself as a main character, made up by his father, A. A.

Charlie Chaplin appears with his mother on the vaudeville stage.

Christina becomes Queen-elect of Sweden.

But now I am six, I'm as clever as clever

So I think I'll be six now for ever and ever.

—A. A. MILNE, *NOW WE ARE SIX*

At the Age of 6 . . .

Wolfgang Amadeus Mozart gives keyboard concerts across Europe.

Shirley Temple receives an honorary Oscar for her contribution to film.

Pepi II becomes Pharaoh of Egypt, a reign that lasts 94 years.

Marie Grosholtz—known later as Madame Tussaud—first works with wax.

Clara Hirschfield, called "Tootsie" by her father, a confectioner, is honored to have his new candy, the Tootsie Roll, named for her.

Warren Buffett, peerless Wall Street investor-to-be, earns profits by selling Coca-Cola to friends.

Marian Anderson, future opera great, joins the junior choir of Philadelphia's Union Baptist Church and learns all the vocal parts of the hymns.

Ron Howard stars as Opie in TV's *The Andy Griffith Show*.

. . . Stephen King writes his first short story.

At the Age of 7 . . .

Helen Keller, blind and deaf, masters a vocabulary of 625 words.

Michael Tan begins studying for a bachelor's degree in mathematics at Canterbury University, New Zealand.

Spock, of *Star Trek* renown, marries in a Vulcan ceremony, during which he bonds telepathically with his bride.

Carol Brown, who travels more than an hour daily to attend a distant school because as a black she is denied admission to the local all-white school, motivates her father to file a lawsuit, resulting in the landmark *Brown v. (Topeka, Kansas) Board of Education* Supreme Court decision which finds public school segregation to be unconstitutional.

Jackie Coogan becomes a millionaire, after appearing in the title role of Charlie Chaplin's *The Kid*.

Yehudi Menuhin, violin virtuoso, solos with the San Francisco Symphony Orchestra.

You should not take a
  fellow eight years old

And make him swear to
  never kiss the girls.

—ROBERT BROWNING, "FRA LIPPO LIPPI"

At the Age of 8 . . .

Virginia O'Hanlon writes a letter to the *New York Sun*, concerned over reports that Santa Claus may not exist, and receives the famous, calming reply—"Yes, Virginia, there is a Santa Claus . . ."

Luis Antonio de Bourbon is elected a cardinal in the Catholic Church.

Joy Foster wins the Jamaican singles and mixed doubles table-tennis titles, making her the youngest-ever national sports champion.

Julie Andrews masters an astounding four-octave singing range.

Evel Knievel witnesses his first motorcycle daredevil jump.

Beatrice Portinari is spotted by Dante Alighieri (age 9), who is so smitten that he will immortalize her later in his *Divine Comedy* as "Beatrice," one of literature's great romantic figures.

Annie Oakley, future sharpshooter, takes her first shot, with her father's old Kentucky rifle.

. . . Genghis Khan becomes chief of his Mongol tribe.

At the Age of 9 . . .

Tutankhamen—King Tut—becomes Pharaoh of Egypt.

Carl "Alfalfa" Switzer joins the *Our Gang* troupe.

Joseph Meister receives the first-ever injection against rabies, from Louis Pasteur.

Natalie Wood stars in *Miracle on 34th Street.*

Kirsen Wilhelm bikes across America, in 66 days.

Maria Agnesi, 18th-century mathematician and philosopher, delivers a one-hour lecture, in Latin, on a woman's right to vote.

Boris Karloff, someday the most famous movie monster ever (Frankenstein's creation), plays the demon king in a children's production of *Cinderella.*

Daisy Ashford writes *The Young Visiters; or Mr. Salteena's Plan,* a novel about Victorian society that will be published to great acclaim and sell over half a million copies.

At the Age of 10 . . .

Gloria Vanderbilt endures a bitter, tabloid-fodder court battle between her mother and aunt to determine custody of the girl and her multimillion-dollar trust fund.

E. B. White writes a poem about a mouse (though he won't write *Stuart Little* for many decades).

Napoleon enrolls in military school.

> **Ah! when I was ten years old I beat you all—Napoleon and all— in ambition!**
>
> —ELIZABETH BARRETT BROWNING, IN A LETTER

Tatum O'Neal wins the Oscar for Best Supporting Actress, for her performance in *Paper Moon*.

At the Age of 10 . . .

George Patton, while playing war games with his cousins, pushes a wagon into a flock of turkeys (which he has deemed the enemy line), killing and injuring many of the birds.

Bessie Smith, "Empress of the Blues," starts singing on the streets of Chattanooga, Tennessee.

George Gordon inherits his great-uncle's estate and acquires the title of Lord Byron.

Anne Lewis wins the Women's Professional Rodeo Association barrel-racing title.

Thomas Edison sets up a laboratory in the basement.

Leonardo DiCaprio is rejected by a talent agent because of a bad haircut.

For the first time in my life—
I was then eleven years old—I
felt myself forced into open
opposition. No matter how hard
and determined my father might
be about putting his own plans
and opinions into action, his son
was no less obstinate in refusing
to accept ideas on which he set
little or no value. I would not
become a civil servant.

—ADOLF HITLER, *MEIN KAMPF*

At the Age of 11 . . .

Anaïs Nin begins making entries in her celebrated diary.

Michael Jackson, lead singer of the Jackson Five, records their huge hit "ABC."

Sonja Henie, Norwegian figure skater, appears in her first Winter Olympics.

Samantha Smith, fifth-grader from Maine, writes a famous letter to Soviet leader Yuri Andropov, asking him why his country wants to rule the world, to which he replies that the USSR wishes to live peacefully with America and others, and invites her to visit.

Charles Miller delivers mail for the Pony Express.

Thomas Gregory, of England, swims across the En-glish Channel.

Marion Morrison inherits the nickname "Duke." (He later changes his given name to John Wayne.)

Anna Paquin wins the Oscar for Best Supporting Actress, for her role in *The Piano*.

Richard Daff, Jr., of Maryland, bowls a perfect 300 game.

At the Age of 12 . . .

Pocahontas saves the life of Captain John Smith, shielding his head with her body so that he will not be put to death.

Tom Sawyer gets his friends to whitewash a fence for him.

Carl Witte earns a Ph.D. in mathematics from the University of Giessen, Germany.

Charles Dickens quits school to work in a factory, pasting labels on bottles of shoe polish, because his father has been imprisoned for debt.

Dolores Haze—better known as Lolita, in Vladimir Nabokov's novel of the same name—drives Humbert Humbert insane with desire.

Cleopatra takes her first lover.

Macaulay Culkin earns $5 million and a percentage of the box office for starring in *Home Alone, Part 2*.

Jesus, with Mary and Joseph, visits Jerusalem for Passover.

. . . Steven Spielberg makes short movies, using his
father's 8mm Kodak camera.

At the Age of 13 . . .

Anne Frank begins her diary, and with her family is soon forced into hiding from the Nazis.

Bill Gates writes his first computer program.

Tycho Brahe witnesses an eclipse of the sun, and is moved to become an astronomer.

Jodie Foster appears in the movie *Taxi Driver*.

Loretta Lynn, future country singing star, marries.

Doris Duke inherits more than $30 million when her tobacco magnate father dies.

Stevie Wonder records the song "Fingertips," his first #1 hit.

Huckleberry Finn, on a raft, floats down the Mississippi River with runaway slave Jim.

Joan of Arc hears voices telling her to help liberate France from English rule.

Dear Diary,
Bobby stole Mary's lunch. I made
him give me the cookies so I wouldn't tell.
Mary's dress was a cheeky shade of blue.

. . . J. Edgar Hoover, paranoid FBI Director-to-be,
starts keeping records in a diary whose cover reads
"Mr. Edgar Hoover, Private."

At the Age of 14 . . .

Nadia Comaneci earns the first perfect "10"—in fact, the first seven of them—ever awarded in Olympic gymnastics competition.

Linda Blair makes heads turn, including her own, in her memorable role in the film *The Exorcist*.

Akbar the Great becomes Mogul Emperor of India.

Bernadette Soubirous, an asthmatic girl from Lourdes, France, experiences visions, is cured of her asthma, tells priests that the Virgin Mary has told her that a chapel should be built there (it eventually is), and inspires pilgrimages to Lourdes.

Wynton Marsalis, trumpet genius, plays with the New Orleans Philharmonic.

John Quincy Adams serves as secretary to the U.S. minister to Russia.

Cheryl Crane, daughter of actress Lana Turner, stabs to death her mother's lover, gangster Johnny Stompanato (alleging he abused and threatened to kill her).

James Maxwell, perhaps the 19th century's greatest physicist, lectures scientists at the Royal Society at Edinburgh about his work in astronomy.

Drew Barrymore writes her autobiography, *Little Girl Lost*.

Andrew Johnson, future American President, serves as a soldier in the Revolutionary War.

Charles III the Simple, son of Louis the Stammerer, succeeds Charles the Fat as King of France.

Ralph Waldo Emerson enrolls at Harvard.

Eric Van Paris invents the cooling fork, which blows cool air onto hot food.

I was a fourteen-year-old boy for thirty years.

—MICKEY ROONEY

At the Age of 15 . . .

Paul McCartney is invited by John Lennon to join his skiffle group, the Quarrymen.

Giacomo Casanova, perhaps history's most famous lover, loses his virginity to two sisters.

Hanson Gregory, a baker's apprentice, pushes the soggy center out of a fried bun and creates the doughnut.

Lana Turner is spied wearing a tight sweater and sipping a soda at the counter of Schwab's Drugstore in Los Angeles, by a Hollywood reporter who will help get her a screen test.

Joe Nuxhall pitches in a major-league baseball game, the youngest to do so.

Sonja Henie wins the first of her three Olympic figure-skating gold medals.

At the Age of 15 . . .

Louis Braille begins devising a system of raised-point writing for the blind to read and write.

Chester Greenwood invents earmuffs.

Pulcheria, daughter of Arcadius, assumes rule over the eastern half of the Roman Empire.

Horatio Nelson, Britain's greatest sea commander, joins the navy.

Brigitte Bardot appears on the cover of French *Elle*.

Joseph-Armand Bombardier, of Quebec, Canada, attaches a Model T engine to his family's sleigh, adds a wood propeller, and invents the snowmobile.

Anne Frank writes in her diary, "in spite of everything I still believe that people are really good at heart"—her third-to-last entry.

At the Age of 16 . . .

Romeo falls for Juliet.

Sybil Ludington, on horseback, warns her Connecticut neighbors for miles around of a coming attack during the Revolutionary War, enabling the colonists to repel the British at Ridgefield.

Arthur Rimbaud writes a new kind of verse, giving birth to Symbolist poetry.

Ella Fitzgerald wins $25 in an amateur singing contest in Harlem.

Henry Ford quits school and takes a job as an engineer.

Angelo Siciliano, a scrawny teen, sees a statue of Hercules at the Brooklyn Museum, joins the local YMCA, begins lifting weights, and starts developing the physique that will make him world famous along with his new legal name, Charles Atlas.

Arthur de Lulli composes "The Celebrated Chop Waltz," better known as "Chopsticks."

At the Age of 16 . . .

Tracy Austin wins the U.S. Open tennis championship.

J. P. Getty III is kidnapped, and when his grandfather, then the world's richest man, refuses to pay the ransom, the boy also loses an ear, which the kidnappers cut off and send to his family to show they mean business. (The ransom is paid, the boy returned.)

Nancy Drew solves a string of mysteries, in the phenomenally popular series of books for teen girls (though in later volumes she will turn 18 so that she may legally drive in any state).

Joseph Conrad, future writer of sea and adventure tales, becomes a sailor.

Lillian Gish ditches her brilliant 11-year stage career to make movies, and becomes perhaps the biggest star of the silent film era.

Cornelius Vanderbilt, future shipping magnate, borrows money to buy a ferryboat.

Buddha marries Yasodhara, his 16-year-old princess cousin.

At the Age of 17 . . .

Judy Garland appears in *The Wizard of Oz*.

Joan of Arc, French army captain, leads her troops against the English, forcing their withdrawal from Orleans, a crucial victory during the Hundred Years War.

Edson Arantes do Nascimento—better known as Pelé—scores six times in the final three tournament games to lead Brazil to its first soccer World Cup.

Holden Caulfield tries to avoid phonies while also finding out where the Central Park ducks go in winter, in J. D. Salinger's *The Catcher in the Rye*.

Ruth Westheimer has her first sexual encounter.

Joseph is robbed of his coat of many colors, then thrown into a pit.

Leslie Hornby, better known as "Twiggy," becomes the world's first supermodel.

At the Age of 17 . . .

Marcel Ravidat stumbles upon the magnificent cave paintings in Lascaux, France, drawn during the Paleolithic period more than 14,000 years before.

Harry Houdini becomes a professional magician.

Marco Polo begins his legendary 24-year expedition through Asia.

Bob Mathias wins the Olympic decathlon.

Aristotle joins Plato's Academy to study philosophy and science.

Howard Hughes inherits his father's machine tool company.

Jim Ryun breaks the four-minute mile, the first high school runner to do so.

At the Age of 18 . . .

Ottaviano is elected Pope (John XII).

Mick Jagger debuts with his new group, the Rollin' Stones.

Jesse James commits his first known bank robbery.

Ansel Adams, who will one day be considered America's greatest nature photographer, gets a summer job at Yellowstone National Park.

Cleopatra becomes Queen of Egypt.

Jennifer Beals stars in *Flashdance*.

Irene Castle, along with her husband, invents the Turkey Trot, a dance that sweeps America.

Emiliano Zapata, Mexican revolutionary, is arrested for leading protests against estate owners.

Victoria becomes Queen of England, a 64-year reign that will make her one of the most beloved monarchs in British history.

Tommy Hilfiger opens his first clothing store, which sells bell-bottoms and other trendy apparel.

. . . Mary Shelley, while vacationing with friends
who have a contest to see who can tell the best ghost
story, starts composing the tale of Frankenstein
and his monster.

At the Age of 19 . . .

Bill Gates cofounds Microsoft.

Gavrilo Princip assassinates Austrian Archduke Ferdinand, the act that ignites World War I.

Patty Hearst is kidnapped by the Symbionese Liberation Army.

Tarzan meets Jane (also age 19).

Barbra Streisand opens to rave reviews on Broadway in *I Can Get It for You Wholesale*.

William Hanna (along with Joseph Barbera) creates cartoon characters Tom and Jerry.

Wayne Gretzky wins the National Hockey League Most Valuable Player Award.

Bob Marley, king of reggae, forms the Wailing Wailers.

Adolf Hitler fails to gain entry, for the second time, to Vienna's Imperial Academy of Fine Arts.

. . . Josephine Baker, exotic dancer-singer, appears in *La Revue nègre,* causing all of Paris to fall in love with her.

At the Age of 20 . . .

David slays Goliath.

Lady Diana Spencer marries Prince Charles of England.

Earvin "Magic" Johnson leads his Los Angeles Lakers to the NBA title and wins the finals MVP Award, though the rookie is not legally old enough to drink champagne in the victorious locker room.

Alexander the Great becomes King of Macedonia and leads the Greeks in war against Persia.

Norma Jean Mortensen is interviewed at 20th Century–Fox Studios, is offered a contract, and is given the name Marilyn Monroe.

Anne Sullivan, the "Miracle Worker," arrives at the Alabama home of Helen Keller to teach the blind and deaf girl to communicate.

Julie Andrews wows audiences in her role as Eliza Doolittle, in the Broadway production of *My Fair Lady*.

Levi Strauss, father of blue jeans, introduces bibless canvas overalls, precursor to his denim version.

At the Age of 20 . . .

Scott Olsen founds Rollerblade, Inc., after buying the patent for an in-line rollerskate, then (along with his brother) improving its design.

Plato becomes a student of Socrates.

K. Switzer runs the Boston Marathon, the first woman officially to do so. (Her first name is Kathy, but she enters as "K." so that the men's-only race will not deny her admission—and she runs even though the race director tries to pull her off the course.)

Antonio de Ulloa discovers platinum.

Tom Cruise stars in *Risky Business*.

This day I *go out of my* TEENS and become twenty! It sounds so strange to me!

—QUEEN VICTORIA, DIARY ENTRY, MAY 24, 1839

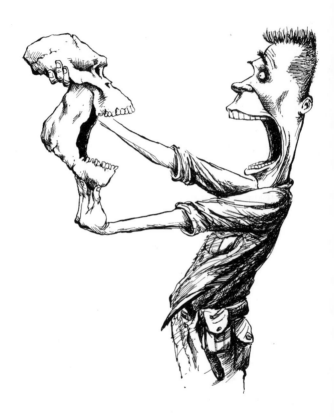

. . . Louis Leakey identifies the skull of
Australopithecus africanus, the first known remains of
ancestors who lived two to three million years ago.

At the Age of 21 . . .

Nathan Hale, American revolutionary caught by the British, laments nobly before his execution that he has "but one life to lose for my country."

Steve Jobs introduces the Apple computer that he and Steve Wozniak created.

Maya Lin, Yale undergraduate, wins a competition to design the Vietnam Veterans Memorial (the unforgettably moving shrine that stands today in Washington, D.C.).

Frederick Douglass escapes slavery.

Jane Austen completes the first draft of *Pride and Prejudice* (it won't be published for 16 more years).

Elvis Presley records "Heartbreak Hotel."

Nathaniel Palmer discovers Antarctica.

Babe Didrikson breaks four track-and-field world records in three hours.

Bonnie Parker, accompanied by Clyde Barrow, begins a two-year string of bank robberies during which 12 people are murdered.

At the Age of 22 . . .

Archimedes, Greek mathematician, cries *"Eureka!"* ("I have found it!") and jumps out of his bathtub when he realizes the law of specific gravity: A body dropped into a liquid displaces an amount of liquid equal to itself.

Norman Rockwell sells his first *Saturday Evening Post* cover.

Charles Darwin begins his historic five-year voyage on the H.M.S. *Beagle*.

Mark Spitz wins seven gold medals in seven swimming events in one Olympics.

Whitney Houston releases her first album, which becomes one of the best-selling debut records ever.

Mark Twain becomes a licensed riverboat pilot.

. . . Ginger Rogers teams with Fred Astaire to make the movie *Flying Down to Rio* and launch the career of America's most loved dance duo.

At the Age of 22 . . .

Cyrus McCormick invents the reaper, thus forever altering farm work and, in fact, world economics, politics, and culture.

Nellie Bly, famously adventurous 19th-century journalist, embarks on a trip around the world to try to beat the 80 days it took Phileas Fogg in Jules Verne's *Around the World in Eighty Days*. (She does it in 72.)

Francis of Assisi falls sick and decides his life would be best spent helping the poor and infirm.

James Boswell meets his hero and life subject, Samuel Johnson, for the first time.

Dick Clark premieres his TV show *American Bandstand*.

Ernest Hemingway moves to Paris, where he will write fiction and hang out with the Lost Generation.

Judith Leyster, the most renowned woman among the Dutch masters, paints *The Proposition*.

Brigitte Bardot stars in the movie *And God Created Woman* and becomes an international sex symbol.

At the Age of 23 . . .

Isaac Newton watches an apple fall from a tree, and is drawn to the subject of gravitation.

Roger Peckinpaugh manages the New York Yankees for 17 games.

Margaret Mead embarks on her first trip to Samoa.

George Fox founds the Quakers, in England.

Marlon Brando takes Broadway by storm, as Stanley Kowalski in *A Streetcar Named Desire.*

Jerry Garcia founds the Grateful Dead.

Daniel Rutherford discovers nitrogen.

Tom Monaghan starts the Domino's Pizza chain.

John Keats, the English poet, writes (among others) "Ode on a Grecian Urn," "Ode to a Nightingale," "To Autumn," "The Eve of St. Agnes," and "Ode on Melancholy," during a single year of artistic ferment almost unequaled (see age 35, Vincent van Gogh).

Jane Taylor writes the nursery rhyme "Twinkle, Twinkle, Little Star."

John Travolta portrays disco king Tony Manero in *Saturday Night Fever.*

At the Age of 24 . . .

Betsy Ross sews the first American flag, at George Washington's request.

Mordecai Anilevitch leads the heroic Warsaw Ghetto uprising in Poland during World War II.

Greta Garbo appears in *Anna Christie,* her first "talkie" ("Garbo speaks!" the posters promise).

Lee Harvey Oswald assassinates President John F. Kennedy.

Jocelyn Bell, an astronomy research student, discovers a pulsar.

James Dean stars in *East of Eden,* one of only three films he will make.

Lorena Bobbitt cuts off most of her husband John's penis.

Georges Seurat begins painting his masterpiece, *Sunday Afternoon on the Island of La Grande Jatte.*

... Chuck Yeager, piloting the Bell XS-1 experimental rocket plane, breaks the sound barrier, the first person to do so.

At the Age of 25 . . .

Charles Lindbergh flies solo across the Atlantic, the first to do so, guiding his plane, *Spirit of St. Louis,* from Roosevelt Field, New York, to Le Bourget Airfield, Paris.

Orson Welles writes, directs, produces, and stars in *Citizen Kane,* revolutionizing film technique.

Dorothy Parker, along with Robert Benchley, starts the Round Table (though it won't be called that until later) of wits and humorists at New York's Algonquin Hotel.

Schoolteacher John Scopes explains evolution to his students, igniting the famous "Monkey Trial."

Roger Bannister breaks the four-minute mile (3:59.4), the first to do so.

Pablo Picasso paints *Les Demoiselles d'Avignon,* the work generally regarded as signaling the birth of "modern art."

No person shall be a representative who shall not have attained to the age of twenty-five years.

—UNITED STATES CONSTITUTION

At the Age of 25 . . .

Samuel Taylor Coleridge descends into an opium-induced trance, writes his dreamy, transcendent poem "Kubla Khan" ("In Xanadu did Kubla Khan / A stately pleasure-dome decree . . . "), then is stirred by a neighbor's knock on the door, thus leaving the work forever unfinished.

Anna Pavlova becomes prima ballerina of Russia's Imperial Ballet.

Booker T. Washington, educator and reformer, founds the Tuskegee Normal and Industrial Institute.

Leonard Bernstein, talented and charismatic assistant conductor for the New York Philharmonic Orchestra, fills in for an ill Bruno Walter, and overnight becomes a star.

Vivien Leigh plays Scarlett O'Hara in the movie *Gone With the Wind.*

Werner Heisenberg announces his revolutionary uncertainty principle.

Roger Ebert becomes film critic for the *Chicago Sun-Times.*

At the Age of 26 . . .

Albert Einstein proposes the special theory of relativity.

Joe DiMaggio hits safely in 56 consecutive games.

Michelangelo completes his spectacularly virtuosic, technically masterful sculpture *Pietà* (see age 88).

Jane Goodall embarks on her first encounter with the chimpanzees of the Gombe Stream Chimp Reserve, at Lake Tanganyika.

Bruce Springsteen appears, in the same week, on the covers of *Time* and *Newsweek*.

Roman Emperor Nero fiddles while his city burns.

At the Age of 26 . . .

Jimi Hendrix performs his famous "Star-Spangled Banner" finale at Woodstock.

Valentina Vladimirova Tereshkova orbits the Earth 48 times in the *Vostok 6,* becoming the first woman in space.

John F. Kennedy acts heroically when his PT boat is sunk by a Japanese destroyer during World War II, helping several members of the crew safely to shore.

Donna Karan assumes creative control of Anne Klein's clothing collection.

John Chapman—better known as "Johnny Appleseed"—starts spreading apple seeds across the Ohio Valley.

Samuel Pepys begins his famous diary.

Joyce Kilmer writes "Trees" ("I think that I shall never see, / A poem lovely as a tree . . . ").

John Wilkes Booth assassinates President Abraham Lincoln.

Lillian Wald, social worker and nurse, helps found the Henry Street Settlement, to help New York City's poor and sick.

At the Age of 27 . . .

Yuri Gagarin becomes the first human in outer space.

Cain kills his brother Abel, then tries to cover up the crime.

Elizabeth II is crowned Queen of England.

Charles Schulz creates the *Peanuts* comic strip.

Adam West debuts as Batman on the TV show.

Elias Howe invents the sewing machine.

Hugh Hefner founds *Playboy* magazine.

Anna Leonowens travels with her son to Siam to be governess to King Mongkut's children (the story will be immortalized by the musical *The King and I*).

Sherlock Holmes meets Dr. Watson for the first time.

Joyce Brothers, pop psychologist, wins the grand prize on TV's *The $64,000 Question* by correctly answering every question from the boxing category.

He was but seven-and-twenty, an age at which many men are not quite common—at which they are hopeful of achievement, resolute in avoidance, thinking that Mammon shall never put a bit on their mouths and get astride their backs, but rather that Mammon, if they have anything to do with him, shall draw their chariot.

—GEORGE ELIOT, *MIDDLEMARCH*

At the Age of 27 . . .

Salvador Dalí paints *Persistence of Memory* (the dripping clocks painting).

Henry David Thoreau moves to the shore of Walden Pond, builds a house, plants a garden, settles into what will be a two-year experiment in simplicity and self-reliance, and starts to record it.

Beatrix Potter sends an illustrated story about a rabbit to a sick child.

Guglielmo Marconi sends the first transatlantic radio message.

Ingrid Bergman stars as Ilsa in *Casablanca*.

Ernest Hemingway publishes *The Sun Also Rises*.

Isadora Duncan, renowned dancer and one of her era's freest spirits, opens a children's dancing school in Berlin.

Steven Spielberg directs *Jaws*.

At the Age of 28 . . .

F. Scott Fitzgerald publishes his greatest novel, *The Great Gatsby*.

Bob Keeshan debuts as Captain Kangaroo.

Julie Andrews stars as Maria von Trapp in the movie *The Sound of Music*.

Carl Bernstein, *Washington Post* reporter, begins investigating the Watergate break-in with Bob Woodward (age 29).

Aimee Semple McPherson, evangelist and faith healer who will gain a huge following, founds the International Church of the Four-Square Gospel, in Los Angeles.

Carl Linnaeus, Swedish botanist, classifies living things according to their structures, revolutionizing taxonomy.

Karen Silkwood drives to meet a newspaper reporter to discuss her alarming allegations that the nuclear power plant where she works uses highly unsafe practices. (She will never meet the reporter, though, because she dies in an automobile crash.)

At the Age of 28 . . .

Lorraine Hansberry writes her affecting drama *Raisin in the Sun*.

Laura Ashley designs scarves at home, the birth of what will become an upscale clothing and home furnishings empire named for her.

Albert Camus publishes *L'Étranger (The Stranger)*.

Judy Holliday plays her most memorable role, in the movie *Born Yesterday*.

Alice Paul founds the Congressional Union for Woman Suffrage (later to be called the National Woman's Party).

David McConnell goes door-to-door selling perfume and building Avon, one day the world's largest cosmetics company.

Fyodor Dostoyevsky faces a firing squad for his political beliefs, but is released at seemingly the last possible moment and told that the terrible fear induced in him is part of the punishment. (He will go on to write *Crime and Punishment*, among other novels.)

... Jackie Robinson plays his first game for the
Brooklyn Dodgers, breaking major league baseball's
color barrier.

. . . Kate Smith sings her signature number, "God Bless America," for the first time; . . . Edvard Munch paints his most well-known work, *The Scream*.

At the Age of 29 . . .

Alexander Graham Bell invents the telephone, his success evident when his assistant hears him, through a receiver connected to a transmitter, say, "Come here, Watson, I want you."

Harriet Tubman, a former slave, starts "conducting" trips on the Underground Railroad to free slaves (she makes 19 trips south, bringing more than 300 slaves to safety in the North or Canada).

J. Edgar Hoover becomes Director of the FBI, a post he will keep until his death 48 years later.

Meriwether Lewis, along with cohort William Clark, leads an expedition in the American Far West.

Martha Stewart buys and renovates a Connecticut farmhouse, and discovers her love for decorating, gardening, and cooking.

George Bernard Shaw loses his virginity.

Mary Quant designs the miniskirt.

At the Age of 29 . . .

Berry Gordy founds Motown.

Jane Addams, leading advocate for the poor and homeless, founds Hull House, the first major social settlement in the U.S.

Michelangelo finishes his sculpture *David*.

Mary Anning, English paleontologist, discovers the remains of a pterodactyl, the first such find of its kind.

Emily Dickinson, poet who would achieve widespread regard and fame only posthumously, retreats from almost all social contact and seriously starts cranking out poems.

Ralph Lauren creates Polo.

Maria Mitchell, self-taught librarian, discovers a new comet, for which she receives international acclaim, and goes on to become America's first professional female astronomer.

At the Age of 30 . . .

Jesus is baptized.

Thomas Edison invents the phonograph. (The first-ever recording is of Edison himself reciting "Mary had a little lamb . . .")

Al Capone, Prohibition-era gangster, authorizes the Valentine's Day Massacre in Chicago, killing his rivals in the bootlegging business.

Dustin Hoffman stars as a recent college graduate in *The Graduate*.

> **We have a saying in the movement that we don't trust anybody over thirty.**
>
> —JACK WEINBERG

Agatha Christie introduces her great Belgian sleuth, Hercule Poirot, in *The Mysterious Affair at Styles*.

At the Age of 30 . . .

Dr. Albert Schweitzer informs his friends that he will soon give up his life of bourgeois comfort and devote himself to helping African natives.

Nat Turner leads a famous slave rebellion in Virginia.

Sylvester Stallone stars in *Rocky*.

Fanny Elssler introduces the polka to America.

Sergeant Alvin York, America's most decorated World War I hero, single-handedly captures 132 German soldiers.

Lisa Marie Presley inherits $38 million from her father's estate.

Ludwig van Beethoven composes the "Moonlight Sonata."

At the Age of 30 . . .

Francisco Vázquez de Coronado, Spanish explorer, discovers the Rio Grande, and introduces horses, mules, pigs, cattle, and sheep to the American Southwest.

Edith Piaf sings "La Vie en Rose."

Sylvia Plath sees her lone novel, *The Bell Jar,* published (then kills herself the following month).

Ivan Pavlov demonstrates, with his studies on dogs, that the stomach produces gastric juices simply in anticipation of food—that is, that animals have "conditioned reflexes."

Scott Joplin publishes his "Maple Leaf Rag."

At the Age of 31 . . .

William Shakespeare writes *Romeo and Juliet.*

Marie Curie, along with husband Pierre, discovers radium.

Bill Gates becomes a billionaire.

Chuck Berry, father of rock and roll, records "Johnny B. Goode."

Shirley Jackson writes the shocking short story "The Lottery."

I shall be thirty-one . . . My youth is gone like a dream; and very little use have I ever made of it. What have I done these last thirty years?

—CHARLOTTE BRONTË, IN A LETTER WRITTEN
JUST MONTHS BEFORE HER NOVEL *JANE EYRE*
IS ACCEPTED, PUBLISHED, AND
BECOMES AN INSTANT SUCCESS

Abbie Hoffman, among others, disrupts the 1968 Democratic National Convention.

Jean-François Champollion, using the Rosetta Stone as guide, deciphers Egyptian hieroglyphics.

Loretta Lynn becomes a grandmother.

Claude Monet paints *Impression: Sunrise,* whose title will be given to the artistic movement with which he and others are associated.

Ellen Futter becomes president of Barnard College.

Florence Nightingale begins her training as a nurse.

Margaret Bourke-White, pioneer in photojournalism, joins the staff of *Life* magazine.

Ralph Nader publishes his cautionary book about the auto industry, *Unsafe at Any Speed.*

Barbara Ruckle Heck, an Irish immigrant, cofounds the Methodist Church in the U.S.

Charles Dickens publishes *A Christmas Carol.*

. . . Herman Melville publishes *Moby-Dick*.

At the Age of 32 . . .

Orville Wright, with brother Wilbur watching, flies a biplane with a 12-horsepower engine for 12 seconds, covering 120 feet, at Kitty Hawk, North Carolina, the moment that gave birth to modern air travel and changed the world forever.

J. D. Salinger publishes *The Catcher in the Rye*.

Sally Ride becomes the first American woman in space, when she flies in the *Challenger* space shuttle for six days.

Bette Nesmith invents Liquid Paper.

Thomas Edison demonstrates the incandescent lamp, igniting the Age of Electricity.

"Shoeless Joe" Jackson, along with other members of the Chicago White Sox, allegedly "throws" the 1919 World Series, even though during the Series Jackson hits .375 and knocks in six runs.

Earvin "Magic" Johnson announces that he is HIV-positive and will retire from playing professional basketball.

At the Age of 32 . . .

Lizzie Borden axes her parents (or maybe not).

Rosalind Elsie Franklin discovers that DNA has a helical structure of two chains, among other features, but Francis Crick and James Watson publish their similar discovery mere weeks before she publishes hers (see age 36).

Harold Ross founds *The New Yorker* magazine.

Franz Kafka publishes his mesmerizing short story "The Metamorphosis."

Chester Carlson, inventor, makes the first Xerox copy.

Thor Heyerdahl sets sail from Peru to Polynesia on his balsa-and-bamboo raft, *Kon-Tiki,* to re-create the vast sea journeys made by primitive peoples.

Lila Wallace, with husband DeWitt, founds *Reader's Digest*.

Sylvia Beach opens the legendary bookstore Shakespeare and Company, on the Left Bank of Paris.

Ali MacGraw appears in *Love Story*.

At the Age of 33 . . .

Thomas Jefferson writes the Declaration of Independence.

Edmund Hillary, with Tenzing Norgay, scales Mount Everest, the first to do so.

George Lucas makes *Star Wars*.

Martin Luther nails to the door of Wittenberg Cathedral his 95 theses, detailing abuses within the Church of Rome and starting the Reformation in Germany.

Wyatt Earp, with Doc Holliday, takes part in the famous gunfight at O.K. Corral.

Catherine Alekseyevna, along with conspirators led by her lover Count Gregory Orlov, pulls off a palace coup against her husband, Czar Peter, enabling her to begin her reign as Catherine the Great.

Jacques Cousteau (with Émile Gagnon) invents apparatus for scuba diving.

**. . . Hermann Rorschach begins research to develop
his inkblot test.**

At the Age of 33 . . .

Amelia Bloomer, editor of a women's rights publication, advocates that women publicly wear less restrictive clothing, like the baggy pants gathered at the ankles that she favors ("bloomers").

Baron Pierre de Coubertin organizes the first modern Olympic Games.

Mary Tyler Moore debuts in her TV show.

James Dewar introduces Twinkies.

Édouard Manet shocks the Paris art world by showing his *Olympia* at an exhibition.

Michelangelo begins work on the Sistine Chapel.

Philip Knight founds his athletic apparel company, Nike.

Lucy Maud Montgomery writes *Anne of Green Gables*.

Mary Wollstonecraft writes the pivotal work *The Vindication of the Rights of Women*.

At the Age of 34 . . .

Martin Luther King delivers his unforgettable "I Have a Dream" speech.

Amelia Earhart flies solo across the Atlantic, the first woman (and second person) to do so.

Napoleon Bonaparte proclaims himself Emperor of France.

Harper Lee writes *To Kill a Mockingbird*.

Andy Warhol creates his image of a Campbell's tomato soup can.

Mildred Hill, kindergarten teacher, composes the music to "Happy Birthday to You."

George Gallup founds the American Institute of Public Opinion, the birth of the Gallup poll.

Elizabeth Taylor gives a memorably brittle performance as Martha in the film *Who's Afraid of Virginia Woolf?*

Captain Bligh faces mutiny by several crew members on his ship, the H.M.S. *Bounty,* and is set adrift in an open boat.

Four years and thirty,
  told this very week,

Have I been now a
  sojourner on earth,

And yet the morning
  gladness is not gone

Which then was in my
  mind.

—WILLIAM WORDSWORTH,
  "THE PRELUDE," BOOK VI

At the Age of 34 . . .

Crystal Lee Sutton, a textile worker, leads the fight to unionize, against much harassment. (Her story is the basis for the movie *Norma Rae*.)

Charles "Lucky" Luciano orders the hit of a rival, then organizes the American Mafia into a collection of "families."

Gustave Flaubert sees his signature novel, *Madame Bovary,* appear in print for the first time, in installments in the *Revue de Paris*.

Emma Lazarus writes some of the most famous lines in American history, now inscribed on a plaque on the base of the Statue of Liberty: "Give me your tired, your poor, / Your huddled masses, yearning to breathe free. . . ."

Edith Head, Hollywood costume designer nonpareil, receives her first screen credit in *She Done Him Wrong*. (The ostrich feather boa that Mae West wears in the movie will become a West trademark.)

Daniel Boone opens the way to the American West by trailblazing through the Cumberland Gap.

At the Age of 35 . . .

Gautama Siddhartha—later known as Buddha—achieves nirvana, awakening, and the peace and tranquility of liberation, while sitting under a bodhi tree.

Joan Anglicus, in male disguise, becomes the only female Pope, John VIII. (Her 2½-year reign ends when she gives birth during a public ceremony.)

William Shatner debuts as Captain Kirk on TV's *Star Trek*.

Alfred Dreyfus, French military officer, is accused and wrongly convicted of treason (a charge overturned, and dismissed as anti-Semitically inspired, 12 years later).

Louisa May Alcott writes *Little Women*, in six weeks.

Tony Bennett records his biggest hit, "I Left My Heart in San Francisco."

Hiram Bingham, American archaeologist, discovers the Inca fortresses of Machu Picchu, near Cuzco, Peru.

Audrey Hepburn stars as Eliza Doolittle in the film version of *My Fair Lady*.

... Vincent van Gogh, in perhaps the single most prolific year experienced by any artist in any field, paints *The Night Café, Artist's Bedroom at Arles, Pink Peach Trees, Café Terrace at Night, Woman Reading a Novel, Garden at Arles,* and on, and on, then cuts off his ear, and keeps painting.

At the Age of 35 . . .

Francis Scott Key writes "The Star-Spangled Banner."

Anita Hill, law school professor, testifies at the Supreme Court confirmation hearings of Clarence Thomas that Thomas made indecent sexual remarks to her when they were colleagues years before.

Henri Charrière—better known as "Papillon"—escapes, incredibly, from Île du Diable (Devil's Island), where he is serving a life sentence.

Johann Sebastian Bach completes the *Brandenburg Concerti*.

Margaret Mitchell publishes her only book, the phenomenally successful *Gone With the Wind*.

Charles Richter develops a scale to measure the strength of earthquakes.

Margaret Rey writes the children's classic *Curious George*.

Svetlana Savitskaya walks in space, the first woman to do so.

At the Age of 36 . . .

William Shakespeare writes *Hamlet*.

Albert Einstein announces his general theory of relativity, revolutionizing physics and astronomy.

Dorothy Hansine Andersen, pathologist, first describes and names cystic fibrosis.

Lech Walesa, Polish electrician, leads a shipyard workers' strike, wins unprecedented rights for a labor group under Communist rule, and forms Solidarity.

Sandy Koufax, former Dodger pitcher, is elected to the Baseball Hall of Fame.

Anne Bancroft appears as Mrs. Robinson in the film *The Graduate*.

Francis Crick, along with James Watson (age 25), discovers the structure of DNA.

Johnny Carson debuts as host of *The Tonight Show*.

At the Age of 36 . . .

Ida Rosenthal, with Enid Bissett, introduces the Maidenform bra.

Katherine Lee Bates writes the words to "America the Beautiful."

Benjamin Franklin invents the Franklin stove.

Gladys Dick, with her husband, founds the Cradle Society, America's first professional child adoption agency.

Edgar Allan Poe publishes his most famous poem, "The Raven."

William Penn, English Quaker leader, founds Pennsylvania.

Gabriel García Marquez writes the beginning of his magical novel *Cien años de soledad (One Hundred Years of Solitude)*.

Estée Lauder sells her first cosmetics, at Saks Fifth Avenue, New York City.

At the Age of 37 . . .

William I the Conquerer defeats Harold II, rival to the English throne, at Hastings.

Ted Kennedy drives off the Chappaquiddick bridge.

James Whistler paints *Arrangement in Grey and Black, Number 1*—more popularly known as *Whistler's Mother*.

Dmitri Mendeleev publishes a periodic table, which arranges the known elements by atomic weight.

King James I commissions a translation of the Bible.

Ann Landers begins writing her hugely popular newspaper advice column.

Martin Luther is excommunicated.

Margaret Sanger opens the first American birth control clinic, in Brooklyn.

WITH A NOD TO HIRSCHFELD

... **George Gershwin premieres his opera,**
Porgy and Bess.

At the Age of 37 . . .

Bernhard Goetz shoots four teenagers on a New York City subway, claiming he felt threatened that they were going to rob him.

Peter Hodgson buys a big lump of soft silicone from General Electric, has small blobs of it packed into clear cases, and sells them, introducing the world to Silly Putty.

Agnes de Mille choreographs her groundbreaking dance piece *Rodeo*.

Anne takes the throne as Queen of England at the start of the 18th century, the last monarch from the House of Stuart.

Amy Tan publishes *The Joy Luck Club*.

Giacomo Puccini premieres his opera *La Bohème,* conducted by Arturo Toscanini in Turin.

At the Age of 38 . . .

Jonas Salk develops the polio vaccine.

Thomas Paine writes *Common Sense*.

Coco Chanel introduces her perfume, Chanel No. 5 (there was no 1, 2, 3, or 4).

Grant Wood paints *American Gothic*, perhaps the best-known American painting.

Gloria Steinem cofounds, and becomes editor of, *Ms.* magazine.

Ann Lee, English mystic, introduces Shakerism, a self-reliant and ultraconservative sect, to America, preaching celibacy and thus pretty much ensuring the movement's limited life span.

Mathew Brady organizes photographic coverage of actual combat in the American Civil War.

Alice McLellan Birney founds what will become the Parent-Teacher Association (PTA).

Patrick Henry delivers his "Give me liberty or give me death" speech, before the provincial Congress in Massachusetts.

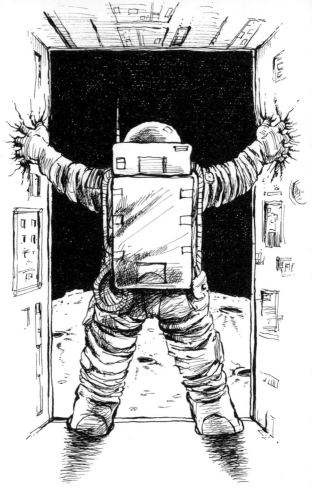

. . . Neil Armstrong walks on the moon.

At the Age of 38 . . .

Ayn Rand publishes *The Fountainhead*.

Benedict Arnold, American Revolutionary War hero, turns traitor, providing American military secrets to the British until he is found out.

Mother Teresa founds the Missionaries of Charity Sisterhood.

Wallace Carothers invents nylon.

Cesar Chavez organizes California grape pickers—mostly migrant, mostly Hispanic—for what will become one of the most effective strikes and boycotts in American labor history.

John Peter Zenger, printer, is acquitted of libel, a landmark triumph for freedom of the press. (Before the case, it was believed that anyone could sue a publisher for printing a negative story, regardless of the truth; Zenger's case showed that the truth *did* matter.)

Grace Brewster Murray Hopper, computer expert who helped devise UNIVAC, coins the term "bug" to describe a computer glitch, when a moth is found inside a machine that doesn't work.

At the Age of 39 . . .

Ferdinand Magellan, Portuguese explorer, begins circumnavigating the globe.

Lao-tzu founds Taoism.

Jean Nidetch, having shed 70 pounds, starts Weight Watchers.

"Bugsy" Siegel begins developing Las Vegas into a gambling mecca.

Teddy Roosevelt leads his Rough Riders to charge San Juan Hill, during the Spanish-American War.

Roald Amundsen reaches the South Pole, along with four other Norwegians, the first known humans to do so.

John Hancock signs the Declaration of Independence.

Dorothy Kunhardt writes and illustrates the tactile children's favorite *Pat the Bunny*.

My thirty-ninth birthday. A good year. I have begotten a fine daughter, published a successful book, drunk 300 bottles of wine, and smoked 300 or more Havana cigars . . . I have about £900 in hand and no grave debts except to the Government; health excellent except when impaired by wine; a wife I love, agreeable work in surroundings of great beauty. Well that is as much as one can hope for.

—EVELYN WAUGH, *DIARIES*

At the Age of 39 . . .

Bing Crosby records "White Christmas," the biggest-selling record ever.

Ellen DeGeneres publicly comes out of the closet.

James Joyce completes what many regard as the greatest novel of the 20th century, *Ulysses*.

Erwin Schrödinger develops his wave theory of sub-atomic particles.

Virginia Johnson, with William Masters, publishes the landmark sex study *Human Sexual Response*.

Jacqueline Kennedy marries again, this time to shipping magnate Aristotle Onassis.

Janet Guthrie drives in the Indianapolis 500 auto race, the first woman to do so.

Leonard Bernstein writes the score for *West Side Story*.

At the Age of 40 . . .

Paul Revere rides his horse to warn the Minutemen of the coming British raid on Concord, Massachusetts.

Brutus, with fellow conspirators, kills Julius Caesar on the Ides of March.

Harriet Beecher Stowe publishes *Uncle Tom's Cabin*.

Mao Tse-tung leads his peasant army on its 6,000-mile Long March.

Hank Aaron hits his 715th home run, more than anyone has ever hit.

Joan Ganz Cooney introduces *Sesame Street* to television.

John Glenn orbits the Earth.

Leo Tolstoy finishes writing his epic, *War and Peace*.

Margaret Rudkin starts Pepperidge Farm, which is also the name of her Connecticut farm, where she bakes whole wheat bread to sell to neighbors.

. . . Joe McCarthy, Republican Senator from Wisconsin,
speaks to a Republican women's club
in West Virginia, and sets off a nationwide
"Red Panic" with his largely fabricated and
ruinous charges of Communist infiltration in American
government and private life.

At the Age of 40 . . .

Bill Wilson, a recovering alcoholic, founds, with his former drinking buddy, Alcoholics Anonymous (AA).

Al Hirschfeld, the great *New York Times* theater caricaturist, begins the tradition of inserting the name of his daughter into his drawings and challenging readers to find all the hidden Ninas.

Mark Twain publishes *The Adventures of Tom Sawyer*.

Lucille Ball debuts in the TV favorite *I Love Lucy*.

Hillary Clinton is named one of America's 100 most influential lawyers, by the *National Law Journal*.

Akira Kurosawa directs his most celebrated film, *Rashomon*.

At the Age of 41 . . .

Columbus lands in the New World (San Salvador in the Bahamas).

Al Jolson appears in *The Jazz Singer*, the first major talking picture.

William Shakespeare writes *King Lear*.

Georgia O'Keeffe spends a summer in Taos, New Mexico, and falls in love with the desert, which serves as the subject of much of her later art.

Joseph Priestley discovers oxygen.

Wilma Mankiller is elected chief of the Cherokee Nation.

Telly Savalas starts shaving his head.

. . . Sigmund Freud analyzes himself.

At the Age of 41 . . .

Emily Davison, English suffragist, protests women's lack of rights by throwing herself in front of the horse of King George V at the Derby, and is trampled to death.

René Descartes pronounces, "Cogito ergo sum" ("I think therefore I am").

Simone de Beauvoir publishes *The Second Sex*.

Mae West says, "Why don't you come up sometime and see me?" in the movie *She Done Him Wrong*.

Sue Grafton writes her first alphabet mystery, *A Is for Alibi*.

Richard Rodgers writes the score for the groundbreaking musical *Oklahoma!*

Plato founds the Academy in Athens, which will exist for almost a thousand years.

At the Age of 42 . . .

Rosa Parks refuses to give up her seat on a Birmingham, Alabama, bus.

King Edward VIII abdicates the British throne for the woman he loves.

Teddy Roosevelt becomes President of the United States, the youngest ever.

Max Planck announces his formula for quantum mechanics.

Ruth Handler, along with her husband, introduces the Barbie doll.

Sigmund Freud stops having sex.

L. Ron Hubbard founds the Church of Scientology.

Humphrey Bogart plays his most famous role, Rick in *Casablanca*.

Marian Anderson, the black opera star, sings at the Lincoln Memorial after being denied by the Daughters of the American Revolution the right to sing at a Washington, D.C., concert hall (a move that prompts Eleanor Roosevelt to renounce her DAR membership).

A boy may still detest age,

But as for me, I know,

A man has reached his
best age

At forty-two or so.

—R. C. LEHMANN, "MIDDLE AGE," *ANNI FUGACES*

At the Age of 42 . . .

Paul Gauguin, post-Impressionist painter, abandons his life in France to sail for Polynesia.

Galileo Galilei invents the compass.

Maria Montessori, educational reformer, opens her first Montessori school, in Tarrytown, New York.

Margot Fonteyn dances for the first time with Rudolf Nureyev (age 24), in *Giselle,* at Covent Garden, London, and they receive twenty-three curtain calls and go on to create a spectacular new dance partnership.

Gregor Mendel, Austrian abbot, publishes his findings on the basic principles of heredity, pioneering the field of genetics.

Ulysses S. Grant, Union general, accepts the surrender of Robert E. Lee, Confederate General, at Appomattox, Virginia, effectively ending the American Civil War.

Betty Friedan writes the pivotal book *The Feminine Mystique.*

Woody Allen co-writes, directs, and stars in the movie *Annie Hall.*

At the Age of 43 . . .

Adolf Hitler is named Chancellor of Germany.

Clement Moore writes " 'Twas the Night Before Christmas."

Alger Hiss is accused of supplying Soviet agents with classified American documents.

Helen Gurley Brown becomes editor in chief of *Cosmopolitan* magazine.

Nostradamus, French astrologer and physician, makes his first prediction.

Dr. Benjamin Spock publishes *The Common Sense Book of Baby and Child Care,* one of the best-selling books ever.

The Fourth Earl of Sandwich—a dissolute aristocrat and gambler who refuses to leave the gaming tables to eat, calling instead for meat and cheese to be brought to him between slices of bread—invents the sandwich.

. . . Thomas Gainsborough paints *The Blue Boy*.

At the Age of 43 . . .

Dr. Virginia Apgar develops the Apgar Score System, a now-standard test administered to infants immediately after birth to assess their well-being.

Anna Edson Taylor survives a plunge over Niagara Falls in a barrel, the first person to make it through alive.

John H. Kellogg, American physician, develops the first flaked cereal.

Diane Arbus enjoys her most successful photographic exhibition—"New Documents" at the Museum of Modern Art—and wins new fans and high regard (but kills herself four years later).

Isabel Perón becomes President of Argentina.

Philip Johnson builds his own famed "Glass House," in New Canaan, Connecticut.

Peter Falk introduces his signature character, Lieutenant Colombo, to TV viewers.

At the Age of 44 . . .

Elizabeth Barrett Browning writes "How do I love thee? Let me count the ways . . . "

Sam Walton founds Wal-Mart.

William Tecumseh Sherman, Union General in the Civil War, begins his famous March to the Sea.

Jimmy Hoffa becomes head of the Teamsters.

Nebuchadnezzar II destroys the First Temple at Jerusalem.

Jennifer O'Neill marries for the seventh time.

Friedrich Nietzsche sees a horse being beaten, runs to embrace it, and loses his mind, never to regain sanity.

O. Henry publishes his most famous short story, "The Gift of the Magi," in *The World*.

Marie Curie wins the Nobel Prize in Chemistry, the first person to win two Nobels.

Jacqueline Susann writes *The Valley of the Dolls,* one of the best-selling books ever.

James Barrie sees his play *Peter Pan* come to life for the first time, on the London stage.

. . . George Washington crosses the Delaware;
. . . "Unsinkable" Molly Brown, passenger on the
Titanic, helps keep spirits up among those on her
lifeboat, commands, rows, and, later on the rescue
ship, helps nurse ill and weak survivors.

At the Age of 45 . . .

Henry Ford introduces the Model T.

Christiaan Barnard, South African surgeon, performs the first successful human heart transplant.

Leonardo da Vinci finishes painting *The Last Supper.*

Betty Friedan cofounds the National Organization of Women.

Walter Cronkite becomes anchorman of the *CBS Evening News.*

Virginia Woolf writes *To the Lighthouse.*

Napoleon Bonaparte attacks British troops at Waterloo, is crushed by the Duke of Wellington, and is exiled to Elba.

Auguste Rodin sculpts one of his most popular works, *The Kiss.*

Gene Roddenberry creates *Star Trek.*

At the Age of 45 . . .

Howard Hughes, billionaire, goes into seclusion, to last the rest of his life.

Charlotte Gulick cofounds the Camp Fire Girls.

John Gotti allegedly rubs out Mafia boss Paul Castellano and his bodyguard, then takes control of the Gambino crime family.

Nathaniel Hawthorne publishes *The Scarlet Letter.*

Jerry Falwell founds the Moral Majority.

Rita Levi-Montalcini helps discover nerve-growth factor, a bodily substance that stimulates the growth of nerve cells.

Martin Klaproth discovers zinc.

Enid Bagnold writes *National Velvet.*

At the Age of 46 . . .

Benjamin Franklin experiments with a kite during a thunderstorm and discovers the presence of electricity in lightning.

Sojourner Truth begins traveling the country, preaching against slavery and for women's suffrage, and developing an excited following across the Northeast and Midwest.

Jack Nicklaus shoots 65 in the final round (30 on the back nine) to win the Masters golf tournament.

Brigham Young, along with many Mormons, arrives at Salt Lake, Utah.

Laura Hobson writes *Gentleman's Agreement*.

Charlie Chaplin begins filming *Modern Times*.

Timothy Leary, Harvard professor and LSD guru, advises America to "turn on, tune in, drop out."

Samuel Beckett writes the monumental play *En Attendant Godot (Waiting for Godot)*.

. . . Peter Minuit buys Manhattan Island for the Dutch from the Canarsie Indian chiefs for beads and goods valued at $24.

At the Age of 46 . . .

Mary Leakey discovers at Olduvai Gorge, Tanzania, the upper teeth and palate of *Zinjanthropus*, thought to be an early hominid.

Charles Darrow invents the game Monopoly.

Michelle Triola sues actor Lee Marvin, her ex-lover, for "palimony," creating a new legal term.

Edward Jenner performs the first inoculation.

Katherine Gibbs starts what will become America's most renowned secretarial school.

William Durant founds the General Motors Corporation.

Mary Robinson is elected President of Ireland, the first woman so honored.

At the Age of 47 . . .

Alexander Fleming, Scottish bacteriologist, discovers penicillin.

William Shakespeare writes *The Tempest*.

Julia Morgan is commissioned by William Randolph Hearst to build his San Simeon castle estate (which she will work on for more than two decades).

Bill Cosby debuts in his smash-to-be TV series *The Cosby Show*.

Reverend Jim Jones coerces 911 followers from his People's Temple, on the island of Guyana, to commit mass suicide by drinking cyanide-laced Kool-Aid.

Virginia Woolf writes *A Room of One's Own*.

Marlon Brando stars as Don Vito Corleone in *The Godfather*.

Auguste Piccard, Belgian physicist, lifts off in his hot-air balloon and becomes the first person to reach the stratosphere.

[Jonathan] Swift was then about forty-seven, at an age when vanity is strongly excited by the amorous attentions of a young woman.

—SAMUEL JOHNSON, *LIVES OF THE POETS*

At the Age of 47 . . .

Joan Collins stars as a bitch-on-wheels in the TV series *Dynasty.*

Antonio Vivaldi composes *The Four Seasons.*

Kate Douglas Wiggin writes *Rebecca of Sunnybrook Farm.*

Frieda Loehmann, with her son, opens a Brooklyn clothing store that will eventually turn into Loehmann's, the national chain of discount stores.

Mel Brooks co-writes, directs, and stars in the movie *Blazing Saddles.*

Dale Carnegie writes one of the first self-help books, the immensely popular *How to Win Friends and Influence People.*

John Dunlop invents the pneumatic tire.

At the Age of 48 . . .

Mark Twain publishes *The Adventures of Huckleberry Finn*.

King John of England signs the Magna Carta, one of history's most influential and admired documents.

Indira Gandhi becomes Prime Minister of India.

Norman Lear creates the TV hit *All in the Family*.

Alfred Binet, French psychologist, devises the first intelligence tests.

Kate Chopin writes the provocative novel *The Awakening*.

Edmund Halley, English astronomer, predicts (correctly) that the comet of 1682 will return 76 years later, though when "Halley's Comet" reappears in 1758, he is no longer around to see it.

Zoë becomes Empress of Byzantium.

Mary Cassatt paints *The Bath*, one of her best-loved paintings of women with children.

Edward Hopper paints *Early Sunday Morning*.

Cardinal Richelieu founds L'Académie Française.

I'll make him an offer that's a winner
I'll put forth a proposal he can't decline
I'm going to strongly suggest...
Oh, c'mon. Please.
This offer good until...

. . . Mario Puzo publishes his hugely popular Mafia
novel *The Godfather*.

At the Age of 49 . . .

Howard Carter discovers the tomb of King Tutankhamen.

Davy Crockett defends the Alamo (but loses his life doing so).

Geraldine Ferraro runs as the 1984 Democratic vice presidential nominee, with Walter Mondale for president, the first woman so represented on a major American party ticket.

Zero Mostel stars on Broadway as the first, and most memorable, Tevye in *Fiddler on the Roof.*

Richard Nixon, after bitterly losing the California gubernatorial election, threatens to give up politics when he informs the press "you won't have Nixon to kick around anymore."

Robert Frost writes his dreamy poem "Stopping by Woods on a Snowy Evening" ("Whose woods these are I think I know. / His house is in the village though . . . ").

Pauline Kael begins her career as movie reviewer for *The New Yorker,* probably the magazine's most famous critic.

Alexander Hamilton agrees to duel Aaron Burr, after Burr hears that Hamilton has slighted him and demands satisfaction. (Hamilton is shot dead.)

At the Age of 49 . . .

Julia Child writes *Mastering the Art of French Cooking,* the bestseller that establishes her on the culinary map.

> **The body is at its best between the ages of thirty and thirty-five: the mind at its best about the age of forty-nine.**
>
> —ARISTOTLE, *RHETORIC*

Henri Rousseau takes early retirement from his job as Paris customs officer to devote himself to painting.

Barbara McClintock, who works with Indian corn rather than standard fruit flies, delivers her controversial paper "Chromosome Behavior and Genic Expression," which explains elements of heredity long before anyone accepts it.

Esther Forbes writes *Johnny Tremain.*

Bram Stoker writes *Dracula.*

At the Age of 50 . . .

Julius Caesar crosses the Rubicon.

Beverly Sills becomes director of the New York City Opera.

Wilhelm Roentgen discovers X-rays.

James Boswell publishes his masterwork, *The Life of Samuel Johnson.*

Bobby Allison, race car driver, holds off fellow driv-er and son, Davey, to win the Daytona 500.

Joy Adamson, champion of preserving African wildlife, writes *Born Free,* about Elsa, the lion cub.

Henry Ford starts the first manufacturing assembly line.

. . . **Charles Darwin publishes**
On the Origin of Species.

At the Age of 50 . . .

William Harvey, British physician, discovers the circulation of blood.

Judith Krantz writes *Scruples.*

Igor Sikorsky builds the first practical helicopter.

Henrik Ibsen writes *A Doll's House.*

Frances Perkins is named U.S. Secretary of Labor—the first female cabinet member and a key author of many of F.D.R.'s New Deal programs.

At the Age of 51 . . .

Sandra Day O'Connor becomes the first woman to serve on the U.S. Supreme Court.

Robert Baden-Powell, British hero in the Boer War, founds the Boy Scouts.

Dian Fossey, zoologist, publishes *Gorillas in the Mist,* about her years in the African rain forest studying the great apes.

Sanctorius, Italian physician, invents the thermometer.

Harriet Monroe founds *Poetry* magazine, which publishes T. S. Eliot, Wallace Stevens, Marianne Moore, and William Carlos Williams, among many others.

Donatien Alphonse François de Sade—the Marquis de Sade—describes, in his novel *Justine; or, The Misfortunes of Virtue,* how sexually gratifying it can be to inflict pain on others.

Gordie Howe scores his 800th National Hockey League goal.

Marshall McLuhan writes, "The medium is the message."

. . . Gail Borden produces condensed milk which does
not sour for three days.

At the Age of 52 . . .

Ludwig van Beethoven composes his *Ninth Symphony.*

Ray Kroc, milkshake-machine salesman, buys out California hamburger chain owners Dick and "Mac" McDonald, and officially starts McDonald's.

Juliette Gordon Low establishes the first troop of Girl Guides in America, which will soon change its name to Girl Scouts.

Jefferson Davis, at the brink of the American Civil War, forms a secessionist government and becomes President of the Confederacy.

Alex Comfort publishes *The Joy of Sex.*

A. C. Nielsen establishes a television rating service.

Jack Ruby kills Lee Harvey Oswald, in front of an entire nation watching on television.

Vladimir Nabokov writes *Lolita.*

. . . Leonardo da Vinci paints the *Mona Lisa*.

At the Age of 52 . . .

Frédéric-Auguste Bartholdi, French sculptor, finishes his design of the Statue of Liberty.

Isak Dinesen publishes *Out of Africa*.

Moshe Dayan is named Minister of Defense and leads Israeli military operations during the Six-Day War.

Pyotr Tchaikovsky composes his beloved ballet suite, *The Nutcracker*.

Harry Houdini, the greatest escape artist ever, stays underwater, in a sealed chamber with only enough air to breathe for perhaps six minutes, for over an hour and a half.

George Eliot publishes *Middlemarch*.

Julius Caesar begins a love affair with Cleopatra, 31 years his junior.

Ayn Rand writes *Atlas Shrugged*.

Constantin Brancusi creates his marvelous abstract sculpture *Bird in Space*.

At the Age of 53 . . .

Abraham Lincoln issues the Emancipation Proclamation, freeing slaves in the Confederate states.

Samuel Morse sends the first telegraphic message ("What hath God wrought?"), from Washington, D.C., to Baltimore.

Margaret Thatcher is elected Prime Minister of Britain, the first woman so elevated.

Walt Disney opens his ambitious dream park, Disneyland.

Dwight D. Eisenhower, Supreme Commander of Allied Forces in World War II, plans and leads the pivotal D-Day invasion at Normandy.

Geraldine Wesolowski gives birth to her grandson. (As surrogate mother, she is implanted with an egg from her daughter-in-law that was fertilized by her son's sperm.)

Ernest Hemingway writes *The Old Man and the Sea.*

Frank Sinatra first sings what will become his signature number, "My Way."

Juan Ponce de León, Spanish explorer, discovers Florida, and plants orange and lemon trees there.

At the Age of 53 . . .

Minnie Minoso of the Chicago White Sox gets a base hit, the oldest major leaguer to do so.

Willa Cather writes *Death Comes for the Archbishop*.

Maurice Ravel comes up with the mesmerizing (some say annoying) theme for *Bolero*.

Corazon Aquino is elected President of the Philippines.

> ## He could hardly be called old at the age of fifty-three.
>
> —FYODOR DOSTOYEVSKY, *THE DEVILS*

Robert James Waller writes *The Bridges of Madison County*.

Lotte Lenya stars in the New York production of *The Threepenny Opera*, playing the role she created 26 years before in Berlin.

Alfred Kinsey publishes *Sexual Behavior in the Human Male*, his provocative landmark study.

At the Age of 54 . . .

Henry Heimlich first describes the choking-prevention maneuver that will be named for him.

Carry Nation, icon of the Prohibition movement, starts smashing saloons with her trademark ax.

Dr. Seuss (Theodor Geisel) publishes *The Grinch Who Stole Christmas.*

Janet Reno is named U.S. Attorney General, the first woman to hold the position.

Bartolomeo Cristofori, of Padua, builds the first known piano.

Bill Shoemaker jockeys 17–1 long shot Ferdinand to a Kentucky Derby victory.

Cass Gilbert, American architect, completes the first modern skyscraper, the 60-story Woolworth Building in New York City.

Vice President Spiro T. Agnew resigns, pleading "no contest" to charges of tax evasion.

... Walter O'Malley, owner of the Brooklyn Dodgers
baseball team, moves them to Los Angeles.

At the Age of 54 . . .

Johanna Spyri writes the children's classic *Heidi*.

Giuseppe Piazzi, Italian astronomer, observes and names the first known asteroid (Ceres).

Sarah Bernhardt, the 19th century's most renowned actress, plays Hamlet.

Dorothy Hodgkin wins the Chemistry Nobel Prize, for determining the structure of vitamin B12.

Theodore Dreiser writes *An American Tragedy*.

Jeane Kirkpatrick becomes U.S. delegate to the United Nations.

Harrison Ford has his ear pierced, something he claims he's wanted to do for a long time.

David Lean directs the epic *Lawrence of Arabia*.

At the Age of 55 . . .

Johannes Gutenberg, inventor of the printing press from Mainz, Germany, publishes the first mass-produced edition of the Bible—300 "42-line Bibles."

Alessandro Volta, Italian physicist, invents the battery.

Pablo Picasso paints *Guernica,* his harrowing mural of the Fascist bombing of the Basque town.

Bobby Riggs loses to Billie Jean King (age 29) in tennis's "Battle of the Sexes."

Ts'ai Lun, Chinese eunuch court officer, invents paper.

Christina Olsen, a disabled Maine resident, poses for Andrew Wyeth's poignant *Christina's World,* one of the most popular American paintings.

Cary Grant stars in Alfred Hitchcock's *North by Northwest*.

Fritz Wankel, German engineer, invents the rotary engine that will be named for him, the biggest improvement in internal combustion engines in more than a half-century.

At the Age of 55 . . .

Rachel Carson, biologist, publishes *Silent Spring,* a warning about rampant pesticide use.

Maimonides, rabbi and physician, writes *Guide of the Perplexed,* the famous 12th-century work that attempts better to unite science, philosophy, and religion.

William Wyler begins filming his spectacle *Ben-Hur.*

Irene Weir, painter, founds the School of Design and Liberal Arts, New York City.

Alex Haley publishes his immensely popular multigenerational epic, *Roots.*

Lorenzo Ghiberti completes his astonishing masterwork *The Gates of Paradise,* one of the finest artistic achievements of the Quattrocento.

Neil Simon writes his comedy *Brighton Beach Memoirs,* the first in his "B" theater trilogy about growing up.

At the Age of 56 . . .

George Handel composes the *Messiah*, in 24 days.

Elizabeth Agassiz starts teaching classes to women in Cambridge, Massachusetts, the seed for what will become Radcliffe College.

Woody Allen is caught, by Mia Farrow, having an affair with Soon-Yi Previn.

Gustave Eiffel completes designing the Paris tower that will be named for him.

Hannah Arendt, historian, writes *Eichmann in Jerusalem* about the trial of the Nazi war criminal, and in it coins the phrase, and articulates the concept of, "the banality of evil."

Confucius resigns as prime minister of the state of Lu to wander, for more than a decade, teaching morals and maxims, including the Golden Rule.

Toni Morrison writes her most acclaimed book, *Beloved*.

General Norman Schwarzkopf leads the Allied forces in the Persian Gulf War.

Mary O'Hara writes *My Friend Flicka*.

At the Age of 56 . . .

Gertrude Whitney opens the doors to the institution she founds, the Whitney Museum of American Art, in New York City.

Norman Mailer writes perhaps his finest work, *The Executioner's Song*.

Olympia Dukakis stars in the movie *Moonstruck*.

Jean Harris, school headmistress, shoots and kills Dr. Herman "Scarsdale Diet" Tarnower, in either a jealous rage or by accident.

Nikolay Rimsky-Korsakov composes the concert staple "The Flight of the Bumble Bee."

> **The general, besides, was in the prime of life—that is, fifty-six, and not a day older, which under any circumstances is the most flourishing age in a man's life, the age at which real life can be rightly said to begin.**
>
> —FYODOR DOSTOYEVSKY, *THE IDIOT*

At the Age of 57 . . .

Émile Zola publishes his famous article *"J'accuse,"* about the Dreyfus affair (see age 35).

George Washington is inaugurated as first President of the United States.

Annie Peck climbs Mount Huascarán in the Andes, the first person to reach the top.

James Joyce publishes *Finnegans Wake*, his most complicated book.

Isoreku Yamamoto, Japanese admiral, devises the surprise attack on Pearl Harbor.

Anna Sewell writes *Black Beauty,* the beloved and best-selling story of a horse.

Jonathan Swift publishes his great satire *Gulliver's Travels*.

Gerardus Mercator, Flemish mapmaker, introduces the world to curved lines on maps to represent longitude and latitude (later called "Mercator projections").

Peggy Wood debuts in *Mama,* the popular 1950s TV series.

LORD CLIP-ON   THE DUKE OF NIGHTIE

. . . The Earl of Cardigan leads the famous Charge of
the Light Brigade, during the Crimean War.

At the Age of 58 . . .

David Livingstone is found east of Lake Tanganyika by Henry Stanley ("Dr. Livingstone, I presume?"), after disappearing five years before in search of the Nile's source.

Karol Wojtyla becomes Pope, John Paul II.

Ellen Hardin Walworth cofounds the Daughters of the American Revolution.

Egyptian President Anwar el-Sadat visits Jerusalem and delivers his historic address to the Israeli Knesset.

Miguel de Cervantes publishes *Don Quixote*.

Ellen Corby appears as Grandma in the TV show *The Waltons*.

John P. Holland invents the first practical submarine, the *Holland VI,* which dives to 75 feet.

W. H. Hoover manufactures a new electric suction sweeper eventually to be known as a vacuum cleaner.

Mary Baker Eddy founds the Church of Christ, Scientist, in Boston.

Louise Nevelson begins to assemble "found objects," pioneering a new form of sculpture.

At the Age of 58 . . .

Didius Julianus, Rome's wealthiest senator, "buys" the Roman Empire at auction. (Unfortunately for him, others are not happy about the auction, and he is murdered soon after.)

Frank Sinatra unretires after two years.

> ### . . . he [Adams] is now fifty-eight, or will be in July . . . all the Presidents were of the same age: General Washington was about fifty-eight, and I was about fifty-eight, and Mr. Jefferson, and Mr. Madison, and Mr. Monroe.
>
> —JOHN ADAMS, FORMER PRESIDENT,
> SPEAKING ABOUT HIS SON, JOHN QUINCY ADAMS,
> WHO HAD JUST BECOME PRESIDENT

At the Age of 59 . . .

Clara Barton founds the American Red Cross.

Leroy Robert "Satchel" Paige pitches in the major leagues (for the Kansas City A's), the oldest ever to appear.

Daniel Defoe publishes *Robinson Crusoe*.

John Brown, abolitionist, leads a famous raid on the U.S. arsenal at Harpers Ferry, Virginia.

Madeleine Albright is named U.S. Secretary of State, the first woman to hold the post.

Edward Hopper paints *Nighthawks* (the lonely patrons sitting in a diner).

Gertrude Stein writes *The Autobiography of Alice B. Toklas*.

Johnny Longden, jockey, wins a race, his 6,032nd, the most ever.

Thomas Bulfinch writes *The Age of Fable,* known later, and quite widely, as *Bulfinch's Mythology.*

Robert Welch founds the John Birch Society.

> **You've got to be fifty-nine years old t'believe a feller is at his best at sixty.**
>
> —KIN HUBBARD, *ABE MARTIN'S SAYINGS*

Edith Wharton wins the Pulitzer Prize for her novel *The Age of Innocence.*

Friedrich Froebel, German schoolteacher, opens the world's first kindergarten.

At the Age of 60 . . .

Thomas Jefferson makes the Louisiana Purchase, paying France $27 million (including interest) for 800,000 square miles that stretch from the Mississippi River to the Rocky Mountains—or about five cents an acre.

Ruth Bader Ginsburg is named to the U.S. Supreme Court.

Alfred Hitchcock directs *Psycho*.

Dom Pérignon whips up sparkling champagne for the first time.

Daniel Carter Beard founds the Boy Scouts of America.

Irma Rombauer, a St. Louis homemaker, writes the phenomenally successful *Joy of Cooking*.

George Papanicolaou gets the medical establishment to recognize that his "Pap" test can help in the early detection of cervical cancer, and save many women's lives.

General William Tecumseh Sherman, Civil War hero, utters his simple, brutal truth: "War is hell."

At the Age of 60 . . .

Hildegard of Bingen, a 12th-century German nun, completes her landmark work, *Physica (Book of Simple Medicine)*, which explains the medicinal value of hundreds of plants and herbs.

W. C. Fields stars in the comedy classic *My Little Chickadee*.

George Eliot, Victorian novelist, marries her broker, 40-year-old John Walker Cross.

> **A man of sixty has spent twenty years in bed and over three years in eating.**
>
> —ARNOLD BENNETT

John Hay, U.S. Secretary of State, proposes his famous Open Door policy, advocating equal privileges for nations trading with China.

Dr. Hattie Alexander discovers the cure for bacterial meningitis.

Groucho Marx debuts as host of his comical TV quiz show *You Bet Your Life*.

At the Age of 61 . . .

Harry Truman decides to drop the Bomb on Hiroshima and Nagasaki, to hasten an end to World War II.

Phineas T. Barnum merges his show with James A. Bailey's to create the world-famous, three-ring Barnum & Bailey Circus, billed as "The Greatest Show on Earth."

Woodrow Wilson announces his 14-point peace plan to end World War I.

Eleanor Roosevelt is elected chairperson of the United Nations Commission on Human Rights and helps draft the Universal Declaration of Human Rights.

Henry James publishes his novel *The Golden Bowl*.

David Ben-Gurion becomes Israel's first Prime Minister.

Jeannette Rankin, Republican Congresswoman from Montana, becomes the lone member of Congress to vote against declaring war on Japan after the Pearl Harbor attack.

. . . Annie Oakley, America's most famous sharpshooter, destroys a record-breaking 98 of 100 clay pigeons in an exhibition at a North Carolina gun club.

At the Age of 62 . . .

Jimmy Hoffa disappears.

Agatha Christie writes *The Mousetrap*, which will become the world's longest-running play.

Douglas MacArthur evacuates from the Philippines during World War II but vows, "I shall return" (and does).

Alec Guinness appears as Ben Kenobi in *Star Wars*.

Eugene V. Debs, labor organizer and socialist, is imprisoned for criticizing the U.S. government.

Nadia Boulanger, arguably the 20th-century's greatest classical music teacher, is appointed director of the American Conservatory.

Louis Pasteur gives a patient the first injection against rabies.

Diana Vreeland accepts the editorship of *Vogue* magazine and quickly becomes a major tastemaker for women's chic.

Henrik Ibsen writes *Hedda Gabler*.

Carl Magee invents the parking meter.

At the Age of 63 . . .

Ferdinand de Lesseps, French engineer, completes work on the Suez Canal.

Arceli Keh, of California, gives birth, the oldest known woman to do so.

Admiral David Farragut issues his celebrated edict, "Damn the torpedoes," as he commands a Union ship to engage the Confederate fleet and cut off Mobile, Alabama's link to the sea.

Anaïs Nin sees the first portions of her provocative diary published.

President Franklin D. Roosevelt attends the conference at Yalta, in the Crimea, to decide with Churchill and Stalin on the endgame of World War II.

Hugh Hefner gives up bachelorhood, again, and weds 26-year-old Miss January 1988.

Voltaire writes his most popular work, the satirical *Candide*.

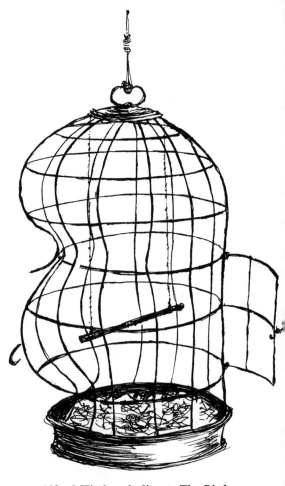

. . . Alfred Hitchcock directs *The Birds*.

At the Age of 63 . . .

Hub Kittle appears in a game for the AAA Springfield baseball team, retiring the side in order in the first inning.

Francis Galton, English eugenicist, shows that no two people share the same fingerprints, thus revolutionizing crime detection.

Dr. Charles Menninger, along with his sons, starts what will become the world-famous Menninger Clinic in Topeka, Kansas, which helps change the way mentally ill patients are treated.

Tomás de Torquemada, the brutally anti-Semitic Dominican monk, takes charge of the Spanish Inquisition and uses unspeakable torture and stake burnings to rid the empire of alleged heretics and others.

Rembrandt van Rijn paints his masterpiece *The Return of the Prodigal Son*.

Leopold Stokowski, conductor, marries 21-year-old Gloria Vanderbilt.

At the Age of 64 . . .

John Pierpont Morgan forms U.S. Steel, the world's first billion-dollar company.

George Washington gives his famous farewell speech.

Oscar Hammerstein II writes the lyrics for *The Sound of Music*.

Betty Ford opens up her self-named clinic for substance abusers.

George Bush pronounces, "Read my lips: No new taxes."

Weller Noble, of California, shoots a 64 on Oakland's Claremont Country Club course—the youngest golfer ever to shoot his age.

Louie Armstrong records "Hello, Dolly."

Ingmar Bergman directs the cinematic valentine to his childhood, *Fanny and Alexander*.

At the Age of 64 . . .

Clara "Mother" Hale takes in the infant of a heroin addict and soon turns her home into Hale House, in Harlem, which takes in and cares for hundreds of babies, many addicted at birth.

Henrik Ibsen writes his play *The Master Builder*.

Harry S. Truman, captured famously on film, gleefully holds up a newspaper trumpeting that his 1952 presidential rival, front-runner Thomas E. Dewey, had beaten him, when in fact Truman had won.

John Napier, Scottish mathematician and father of the decimal point, introduces his new invention, the logarithm.

At the Age of 65 . . .

William Henry Seward, U.S. Secretary of State, buys from Russia's Czar Alexander II the 580,000 square miles that make up Alaska, for $7,200,000—or less than two cents an acre.

Laura Ingalls Wilder publishes *Little House in the Big Woods,* the first of her popular eight-volume *Little House on the Prairie* series (made more popular by the TV show).

Colonel Harland Sanders drives around the country, looking to license his special "finger-lickin' good" chicken recipe, and starts to build what will become the Kentucky Fried Chicken empire.

James Monroe enunciates his "Monroe Doctrine," establishing a we-mind-our-business-and-you-mind-yours American foreign policy.

Fran Lee, New York activist, helps push through the City Council the "Pooper Scooper" law, requiring dog owners to clean up after their pets when walking them.

Judah ha-Kadosh compiles the *Mishnah,* which helps to establish Jewish Talmudic law.

William Jennings Bryan, three-time U.S. presidential nominee and fundamentalist, represents the state's creationist case in the famous Scopes "Monkey Trial."

George Cukor directs *My Fair Lady*.

Elizabeth Hazen announces her discovery, along with Rachel Brown, of mystatin, a safe fungicide which may be used to treat life-threatening diseases, ringworm, athlete's foot, Dutch elm disease, and more.

Andrew Carnegie sells Carnegie Steel to U.S. Steel for hundreds of millions of dollars, and begins in earnest what will be his more enduring legacy: philanthropy.

Winston Churchill becomes Britain's Prime Minister.

C. Everett Koop, the U.S. Surgeon General, issues his report calling cigarette smoking the chief preventable cause of death.

Mary Leakey discovers 3.5-million-year-old fossilized footprints in Tanzania.

Henry Moore sculpts his famous reclining figure, which sits in Lincoln Center, New York City.

At the Age of 66 . . .

Secretary of State George Marshall announces his post-World War II European Recovery Program—the economic aid package better known as "The Marshall Plan."

Michelangelo completes the *Last Judgment* fresco in the Sistine Chapel.

Annie Jump Cannon, astronomer, completes her catalog of stars, accounting for 400,000 celestial objects.

Spencer Tracy stars in *Guess Who's Coming to Dinner.*

Carrie Fuld cofounds the Institute for Advanced Study at Princeton, the prestigious facility where Einstein and others will come to think and work.

Henry Cavendish calculates the gravitational constant, making it possible to determine Earth's mass.

Nikos Kazantzakis writes *Zorba the Greek.*

Maggie Kuhn founds the Gray Panthers.

At the Age of 67 . . .

Joseph Baermann Strauss, engineer, sees his most stunning work—the Golden Gate Bridge—open to traffic.

Louise Boyd flies over the North Pole, the first woman to do so.

John Rock, gynecologist, begins extensive testing of the birth control pill.

Aeschylus writes his masterpiece, the *Oresteia* trilogy.

Ellen Browning Scripps establishes the Marine Biological Association in San Diego, California, which later becomes the world-famous Scripps Institution of Oceanography.

George Bernard Shaw writes *Saint Joan.*

Ernest Vincent Wright writes *Gadsby,* a novel that does not use the letter "e."

Lloyd Bentsen, 1988 Democratic vice presidential nominee, memorably informs his TV debate rival, Dan Quayle, "Senator, you are no Jack Kennedy."

At the Age of 68 . . .

Clarence Darrow, one of America's greatest trial lawyers, defends John Scopes for teaching evolution in schools, in the famous Tennessee "Monkey Trial."

Nikita Khrushchev places intermediate-range nuclear missiles in Cuba, thus setting off the Cuban Missile Crisis.

Russell Baker replaces Alistair Cooke as host of PBS's *Masterpiece Theatre.*

Clifford Batt, of Australia, swims the English Channel.

Lillian Carter (mother of President Jimmy Carter) joins the Peace Corps, and for two years works as a nurse outside Bombay, India.

Clodion, noted French sculptor, begins work on a massive frieze on the Arc de Triomphe, Paris.

Mary Harris "Mother" Jones helps found the Social Democratic Party.

At the Age of 68 . . .

Henry Miller finally enjoys the American publication of his novel *Tropic of Cancer*, banned in the U.S. for 27 years.

Lionel Barrymore appears as mean old Mr. Potter in *It's a Wonderful Life*.

Giotto di Bondone begins work on the famous Campanile in Florence.

Francisco (José) de Goya y Lucientes—Goya, to most—paints his famous *The Third of May, 1808*.

Victor Hugo returns to France after 19 years in political exile.

Edna Ernestine Kramer Lassar, mathematician and teacher, publishes her most important work, *The Nature and Growth of Modern Mathematics*.

At the Age of 69 . . .

A. C. Bhaktivedanta founds the International Society for Krishna Consciousness (Hare Krishnas).

Neville Chamberlain, British Prime Minister, makes one of the century's most misguided decisions by signing the Munich Agreement with Adolf Hitler, thus allowing the Nazis to annex Czechoslovakia and helping to set the stage for World War II.

Mother Teresa wins the Nobel Peace Prize.

Francis Chichester sails solo across the Atlantic Ocean—4,000 miles in 22 days.

Boutros Boutros-Ghali is named Secretary General of the United Nations.

Richard Wagner composes his opera *Parsifal*.

Laurence Olivier gives arguably his most chilling performance in the film *Marathon Man,* much to the chagrin of the dental profession.

At the Age of 69 . . .

Noah Webster publishes *An American Dictionary of the English Language,* which he has worked on for 22 years and which will become one of the best-selling books of all time.

Maurice Chevalier sings "Thank Heaven for Little Girls," in the movie *Gigi.*

Linus Pauling reports that vitamin C, in high doses, may help prevent the flu and common cold—a prescription that defies much existing wisdom.

Donato di Niccolò di Betto Bardi—better known as Donatello—completes his breathtaking painted-wood sculpture of Mary Magdalen.

Brigham Young fathers his 56th, and last, child.

At the Age of 70 . . .

Socrates is condemned to die for corrupting the minds of Athenian youth.

Golda Meir is elected Prime Minister of Israel.

Nicolaus Copernicus publishes, after 30 years of work, *De revolutionibus orbium coelestium (On the Revolution of the Celestial Spheres)*, which posits that the Sun, not the Earth, is at the center of the cosmos, the principle that gives birth to modern astronomy.

Dr. William Worrall Mayo founds his famous medical clinic.

E. B. White writes the children's classic *The Trumpet of the Swan*.

Marguerite Duras writes *The Lover*.

Shigechiyo Izumo takes up smoking for the first time. (He will live to 120.)

Elizabeth Gurley Flynn becomes head of the U.S. Communist Party, the first woman to do so.

Somerset Maugham writes *The Razor's Edge*.

At the Age of 71 . . .

Coco Chanel introduces the Chanel suit.

Nelson Mandela is released from a South African prison, after 27 years' incarceration.

Joe Sweeney becomes a member of the Salem (Massachusetts) State College tennis varsity.

Winston Churchill coins the term "Iron Curtain."

Ambrose Bierce, popular and caustic journalist, disappears mysteriously.

Buckminster Fuller builds his largest geodesic dome, for the U.S. Pavilion at Expo 67, in Montreal.

John Houseman wins an Oscar for Best Supporting Actor, for his performance as the stern law professor in *The Paper Chase*.

Aurelius Augustinus—Christian philosopher later known as St. Augustine—finishes writing *The City of God*.

Euripides writes his play *Electra*.

At the Age of 72 . . .

Sophocles writes probably his greatest play, and one of the greatest written by anyone, *Oedipus Rex*.

Michelangelo designs the dome of St. Peter's Basilica, Rome.

Mary Randolph writes *The Virginia Housewife,* America's first regional cookbook.

Daniel Chester French, sculptor, completes the marble figure of Abraham Lincoln seated in the Lincoln Memorial.

King George III, who ruled England while its American colony fought for, then won, its independence, goes mad.

Karl Wallenda, one of the century's most celebrated tightrope walkers, walks a high wire between the Eden Roc and Fontainebleau hotels in Miami.

The Marquis de Sade takes a new, 15-year-old lover.

Thomas Mann completes his ambitious and tragic novel *Doktor Faustus*.

Oscar Swahn wins an Olympic silver medal in the shooting competition.

Betty Friedan writes *The Fountain of Age*.

. . . Peter Mark Roget finishes compiling his *Thesaurus,* after twelve years of work.

At the Age of 73 . . .

Ronald Reagan is reelected President of the United States.

Madame Tussaud, modeler in wax, establishes a permanent London home for her world-famous exhibition of life-size models and chamber of horrors.

Earl Warren, Chief Justice of the Supreme Court and head of the Warren Commission, releases its report on J. F. K.'s assassination, ruling that there was no conspiracy.

Lee Strasberg, arguably the greatest acting teacher of his time, himself gives his most memorable acting performance, as Hyman Roth in *The Godfather, Part 2*.

Albert Einstein is offered, and declines, the presidency of Israel.

Walt Stack completes the Ironman Triathlon in 26 hours, 20 minutes.

Bertrand Russell publishes his massive and brilliant *A History of Western Philosophy*.

At the Age of 74 . . .

Albert Einstein announces his unified field theory (it does not hold up).

Julius Hoffman presides over the famously chaotic trial of the Chicago Seven.

Ethel Andrus founds the American Association of Retired Persons (AARP).

John D. Rockefeller donates $100 million to the Rockefeller Foundation, to that point the single largest philanthropic gesture ever.

Cass Gilbert designs the U.S. Supreme Court Building.

Titian completes his masterpiece *Rape of Europa*.

Glikl Hamil, a 17th-century German housewife, finishes writing *Zikhroynes mores Glikl Hamil (The Life of Glückel of Hameln),* an account of her life raising 14 children that will come to be regarded as the first work of modern Yiddish literature.

Claude Monet starts painting what will become his celebrated panels of water lilies.

At the Age of 75 . . .

Cecil B. DeMille directs *The Ten Commandments* (remaking the movie he directed a third of a century before).

Mary Harris "Mother" Jones, labor leader extraordinaire, helps found the Industrial Workers of the World.

George Everest, former Surveyor General of India who measured the highest peak in the world (formerly called Peak XV), is pleased to have it renamed in his honor, Mount Everest.

> **There can be a rewarding relationship between the sevens and the seventy-fives. They are both closer to the world of mythology and magic than all the busier people between those ages.**
>
> —J. B PRIESTLEY, *GROWING OLD*

At the Age of 75 . . .

Ruth Gordon appears in *Harold and Maude*.

Luke Appling, playing in an Old-Timers' Game at Washington's RFK Stadium, hits a home run off of Warren Spahn.

Claudio Arrau, one of the world's great piano virtuosos, gives 110 concerts.

Fanny Garrison Villard founds the Women's Peace Society.

Ferdowsi writes *Shah-nameh* (Book of Kings), the Persian national epic poem.

Akira Kurosawa wraps shooting on *Ran,* his take on *King Lear*.

William Paley helps found the Museum of Broadcasting in New York City.

At the Age of 76 . . .

Thomas Jefferson starts designing the buildings and curriculum of the University of Virginia.

Marguerite Yourcenar, the writer, becomes the first woman elected to L'Académie Française since it was founded 345 years before.

Charles Foster Kane, of *Citizen Kane,* whispers his immortal, confounding clue, "Rosebud."

Henry Fonda stars in *On Golden Pond.*

Clara Barton, founder of the American Red Cross, rides mule wagons and performs nursely duties during the Spanish-American War.

Auguste Rodin finally marries his lifelong companion, Rose Beuret, whom he met when he was 23 and she 20.

Angelo Giuseppe Roncalli is elected Pope—John XXIII—one of the most popular ever.

Gilbert Murray, classics scholar from Oxford University, founds the organization Oxfam to help fight world hunger.

Bernard Baruch coins the term "cold war."

(Actual size)

... Senator Sam Ervin, Jr., Democrat from North
Carolina, chairs the committee investigating the
Watergate affair.

At the Age of 77 . . .

Mahatma Gandhi fasts to quell religious violence in India.

John Glenn returns to space, after an absence of several decades.

Benjamin Franklin helps win official British recognition of American independence.

Louise Nevelson designs the interior of the Chapel of the Good Shepherd, in St. Peter's Church, New York.

Luis Buñuel directs the film *That Obscure Object of Desire*.

Juan Perón, former dictator of Argentina, returns to his homeland after 18 years in exile.

Giovanni Giolitti is elected Prime Minister of Italy for the fifth time.

Andrés Segovia, classical guitarist, enjoys the birth of his son Carlos.

Thornton Wilder writes the novel *Theophilus North*.

I can hardly think I am entered this day into the seventy-eighth year of my age. By the blessing of God, I am just the same as when I entered the twenty-eighth. This hath God wrought, chiefly by my constant exercise, my rising early, and preaching morning and evening.

—JOHN WESLEY, *JOURNALS*

At the Age of 78 . . .

Ayatollah Ruholla Khomeini, having fomented a revolution from afar, returns to Iran after 15 years in exile, and assumes power.

Eleanor of Aquitaine leads an army to crush a rebellion by her grandson (Arthur, the Duke of Brittany) against her son (John, the King of England).

Oliver Wendell Holmes, Jr., Supreme Court Justice and champion of free speech, delivers his most famous exception, opining that the right to free speech "would not protect a man in falsely shouting fire in a theater and causing a panic."

Georgia O'Keeffe paints *Sky Above Clouds IV*.

Euripides writes his masterpiece *Bacchae*.

Sam Rayburn, legendary Democratic Congressman from Texas, is reelected Speaker of the House.

Richard Strauss finishes composing his opera *Capriccio*.

H. G. Wells, who dropped out of school at age 14, earns his doctorate from London University.

. . . Grandma Moses takes up painting seriously.

At the Age of 79 . . .

Benjamin Franklin invents bifocal eyeglasses.

Christopher Wren, British architect, officially completes the spectacular St. Paul's Cathedral, London, which he has worked on for 35 years.

Katherine McCormick helps to fund the Worcester Foundation, which does groundbreaking work in treating the mentally ill.

George Cayley engineers the first manned, heavier-than-air flight (a half century before the Wright Brothers) when a glider carries his coachman 1,500 feet over a valley.

Marc Chagall unveils his murals at New York City's Metropolitan Opera House.

Giuseppe Verdi composes his opera *Falstaff*.

Cornelius Vanderbilt okays construction of Grand Central Terminal in New York, creating thousands of jobs.

John Knight merges his newspapers with Ridder's, creating the Knight-Ridder chain.

Emily Greene Balch, cofounder of the Women's International League for Peace and Freedom, wins the Nobel Peace Prize.

. . . Moses encounters the burning bush.

At the Age of 80 . . .

Moses, in disgust, breaks the tablets inscribed with the Ten Commandments, then goes back to get a second set.

Queen Victoria utters her famous critique, "We are not amused."

Jessica Tandy wins her first Oscar, for Best Actress in *Driving Miss Daisy*.

George Burns *also* wins his first Oscar, for Best Supporting Actor in *The Sunshine Boys*.

Pope Gregory XIII establishes the Gregorian calendar, thus correcting the errors in the Julian calendar. (He does this by making the day following October 4, 1582, be October 15, 1582, and by changing rules governing leap years.)

Robert Penn Warren becomes America's first official poet laureate.

Leopold Stokowski founds the American Symphony Orchestra.

In a dream you are never eighty.

—ANNE SEXTON, "OLD," *SELECTED POEMS*

At the Age of 81 . . .

Amos Alonzo Stagg is named football college coach of the year.

Barbara McClintock wins the Nobel Prize for Physiology or Medicine, for her revolutionary work in genetics.

Jerry Wehman, of Florida, bowls a perfect 300 game.

Alessandro Pertini becomes Italy's first socialist President.

John Huston directs *The Dead*.

Fred Astaire marries 37-year-old jockey Robyn Smith.

J. Paul Getty opens the spectacular Getty Museum, in Malibu, California.

At the Age of 82 . . .

Charlie Chaplin returns to the United States, after twenty years of exile for his political beliefs, to receive a special Oscar award.

Henri Matisse creates *The Swimming Pool,* one of the finest examples of his "cutout" art.

Thelma Pitt-Turner completes the Hastings (New Zealand) Marathon in 7 hours, 58 minutes.

Johann Wolfgang von Goethe completes his masterpiece *Faust*.

James Cagney appears in the movie *Ragtime*.

William Gladstone becomes British Prime Minister for the fourth, nonconsecutive time.

George Bernard Shaw wins the Best Screenplay Oscar for *Pygmalion* (making him the only person ever to win both a Nobel Prize and an Academy Award).

Andrew Mellon donates much of his phenomenal art collection to the U.S. government, then kicks in another $15 million to build a place to put it—the National Gallery of Art, in Washington, D.C.

At the Age of 83 . . .

Winston Churchill publishes the last of four volumes of his ambitious *A History of the English-Speaking Peoples*.

Benjamin Spock is arrested for demonstrating against the Vietnam War.

Igor Stravinsky composes his *Requiem Canticles*.

Sigmund Freud writes *Moses and Monotheism*.

Samuel Smith, War of 1812 hero, takes charge of the Maryland state militia to repel riots in Baltimore (in thanks, the city will elect him mayor).

. . . Giovanni Bellini, Renaissance painter, completes one of his masterpieces, *St. Jerome with St. Christopher and St. Augustine*.

At the Age of 84 . . .

Henri Pétain becomes head of the collaborationist Vichy government in France.

> **I, personally, have succeeded in living nearly eighty-five years without taking any trouble about my diet.**
>
> —BERTRAND RUSSELL

Pablo Casals gives a famous cello recital at the Kennedy White House.

Andrea Doria, foremost naval commander of his time, sails against the Barbary pirates.

Avery Brundage, head of the International Olympic Committee, refuses to stop the 1972 Munich Olympics after 11 Israeli athletes are murdered by terrorists.

Lydia Yeamans Titus makes her screen debut in Rudolph Valentino's *All Night*.

At the Age of 85 . . .

Bertrand Russell introduces the international peace symbol.

Celestine III is elected Pope.

Paul von Hindenburg, President of Germany, appoints Adolf Hitler as Chancellor.

At the Age of 86 . . .

Robert Frost recites his new poem, "The Gift Outright," at the presidential inauguration of John F. Kennedy.

Jean Lowrie founds the International Association of School Librarians.

Thomas Hobbes translates Homer's *Odyssey*.

At the Age of 87 . . .

Mary Baker Eddy founds *The Christian Science Monitor*.

Sophocles writes his play *Philoctetes*.

Jeannette Rankin, the first female member of Congress and the only one to vote against declaring war on Japan after the Pearl Harbor attack, leads an anti-Vietnam protest on Capitol Hill.

John Gielgud appears in the film *Prospero's Books*.

Francis Peyton Rous, American pathologist, wins the Nobel Prize for Chemistry for his work in discovering viruses that cause cancer.

At the Age of 88 . . .

Michelangelo crafts perhaps his most heartbreaking sculpture, the *Rondandini Pietà*—an old man holding Christ, spare and simple—which is dramatically different from the magnificent *Pietà* the artist sculpted in his early twenties (see age 26).

Helen Hooven Santmyer enjoys sudden fame with her surprise best-seller . . . *And Ladies of the Club.*

Sofonisba Anguisciola, Italian Renaissance painter and the first female artist to gain world renown, creates *Self-Portrait.*

Lise Meitner, Austrian physicist, wins the Enrico Fermi Prize for her work in nuclear fission.

Margaret Olivia Slocum Sage founds the Russell Sage College for Women.

At the Age of 89 . . .

Frank Lloyd Wright completes work on the Guggenheim Museum.

Eubie Blake, jazz-piano great, starts his own publishing and recording company.

Will Durant, along with wife Ariel, publishes *The Age of Napoleon,* the eleventh volume of their epic history, *The Story of Civilization.*

Artur Rubinstein performs one of the most renowned concerts of his classical piano career, at New York's Carnegie Hall.

Mary Somerville—Scottish geologist, astronomer, and mathematician—writes *On Molecular and Microscopic Science.*

Edmond Hoyle, perhaps the world's leading authority on card games, now pens a treatise on chess.

. . . Corena Leslie parachutes over Buckeye Airport in
Sun Valley, Arizona.

At the Age of 90 . . .

Sophocles writes one of the great dramas in history, *Oedipus at Colonus*.

Edith Hamilton, popularizer of classical Greek literature, is made an honorary citizen of Athens.

Jacob Coxey, who 50 years before had led a group of unemployed workers—called "Coxey's Army"—on a five-week march, on foot, from Ohio to Washington, D.C., to demand federal aid for public works, only to be arrested upon his arrival on the Capitol lawn for trespassing . . . finally gets to deliver the speech he had meant to deliver.

. . . Sarah gives birth to her only child, Isaac.

At the Age of 91 . . .

Maude Tull, of California, gets her first driver's license.

Hulda Crooks climbs Mount Whitney, the highest peak in the continental United States.

> **I did affirm to my readers in *My Young Years* that I was the happiest man I had ever met and I can profoundly reaffirm it at the age of ninety-one.**
>
> —ARTUR RUBINSTEIN, *MY MANY YEARS*

At the Age of 92 . . .

George Burns, portraying an 81-year-old, appears in the movie *18 Again*.

Havergal Brian, British composer, pens his 33rd symphony.

George Bernard Shaw writes *Shakes Versus Shav: A Puppet Play*.

P. G. Wodehouse completes yet another Jeeves book, *Aunts Aren't Gentlemen*.

At the Age of 93 . . .

Strom Thurmond, Republican Senator from South Carolina, is reelected again, sending him to Washington for his eighth term.

Lillian Gish stars in *The Whales of August* 72 years after starring in *The Birth of a Nation*.

At the Age of 94 . . .

Leopold Stokowski, conductor, signs a 6-year recording contract.

At the Age of 95 . . .

Martha Graham premieres her latest choreographed work, *Maple Leaf Gala*.

Mother Jones, union organizer, writes her autobiography.

Now that I am ninety-five years old, looking back over the years, I have seen many changes take place, so many inventions have been made, things now go faster, in olden times things were not so rushed. I think people were more content, more satisfied with life than they are today, you don't hear nearly as much laughter and shouting as you did in my day, and what was fun for us wouldn't be fun now . . .

—GRANDMA MOSES (1955)

At the Age of 96 . . .

Amos Alonzo Stagg, football coaching great, appears on the cover of *Time* magazine.

Pablo Casals conducts the Israel Festival Youth Orchestra performing a Mozart symphony.

At the Age of 97 . . .

Simon Stern, of Wisconsin, is divorced from his wife, 91-year-old Ida.

At the Age of 98 . . .

Dimitrion Yordanidis runs a marathon, in Athens, Greece, in 7 hours, 33 minutes.

At the Age of 99 . . .

Otto Bucher scores a hole-in-one on the 12th hole (130 yards long) at Spain's La Manga golf course.

. . . At the age of 99, Abraham circumcises
himself.

At the Age of 100 . . .

Gwen Ffrangcon-Davies, legendary British stage actress for eight decades, appears in the movie *The Master Blackmailer,* and is also made a Dame by the Order of the British Empire.

Ichijirou Araya climbs Mount Fuji.

ANDREW POSTMAN, 38—the age at which Neil Armstrong walked on the Moon—is the author of three previous books, including *Now I Know Everything,* a novel. His work has appeared in numerous publications, including *The New York Times, The Washington Post, Diversion,* and *GQ,* among others, and he was a columnist for several years for *Glamour.* A co-founder of Smart Games, Inc., he lives in New York with his wife and newborn son.

NICK GALIFIANAKIS is a freelance illustrator whose work appears in *The Washington Post*'s nationally syndicated column "Tell Me About It" and in other major publications. He lives with his wife and Zuzu, his dog.